ADVANC

SHELTER FO

"A full-throttle descent into visceral terror, *Shelter for the Damned* grabs you by the throat and never lets go. This haunting tale heralds the arrival of Mike Thorn as a horror writer to watch." —Jeffrey Reddick, creator of *Final Destination*

"A terrifying descent into suburban addiction and male shame, *Shelter for the Damned* is a gripping, uncanny tale cut from the same cloth as Stephen King and John Carpenter." —Daniel Goldhaber, director of *Cam*

"Mike Thorn's debut novel, *Shelter for the Damned*, is an intimate, slow burn exploration of troubled teenager Mark as he stumbles through dysfunction that distorts his interactions with family and friends, as well as his own thoughts. Throughout, an insidious menace percolates beneath, initiated by the discovery of a mysterious shack that might not be what it seems. Every strain for normality is upended; every course of action Mark takes devolves into violence and death… and horrors beyond that, all laced with genuine terror. The shadowy truth of Mark's circumstances and the addictive influence of the shack lead him and the reader to a harrowing, surreal finale that left my jaw on the floor. Impressive is an understatement. Mike Thorn is a fresh voice in horror with a distinct vision well worth your attention." —John Claude Smith, author of *Occasional Beasts: Tales* and the Bram Stoker Award® nominated *Riding the Centipede*

"Like a more mature *Stranger Things*, Mike Thorn's debut coming-of-age novel turns everyday adolescent experiences into the stuff of nightmares. The protagonist, Mark, is both enigmatic and terrifying as he encounters forces beyond his control in an abandoned shack, threatening his relationships and his grip on reality. *Shelter for the Damned* is a genre standout, among the likes of King's *The Body*. It is a gripping read that won't let you sleep even after you've read the final words." —Erin Emily Ann Vance, author of *Advice for Taxidermists and Amateur Beekeepers*

"A twisted and twisting tale of male adolescence in all its granular horror—the small resentments, the misrecognitions, the petty power plays, the inchoate longing, the misdirected rage, the unexpected violence, and, most of all, the final failure to make meaning of all this teenage chaos—so many night terrors come together in this absorbing literary horror by Mike Thorn." —Randy Nikkel Schroeder, author of *Arctic Smoke*

"A lucid suburban nightmare. Richly textured, visceral and haunting, *Shelter for the Damned* will unearth fears you didn't even know you had." —Niall Howell, author of *Only Pretty Damned*

"We all need a place of shelter. Mike Thorn asks us, 'What if your cherished sanctuary isn't what it seems?' In their iconic song 'Subdivisions,' Canadian rock band Rush sang, 'The suburbs have no charms to soothe the restless dreams of youth.' Thorn taps into the rage of suburban youth with this tale of high school friends, bullies, and parents who don't understand. And of course there are monsters, and murder, in *Shelter for the Damned*; the only question left is, will you take the ride Mike Thorn has in store for you and take shelter there?" —Daniel Braum, author of *Underworld Dreams*

Shelter
for the
DAMNED
MIKE THORN

JOURNALSTONE
YOUR LINK TO ARTIST TALENT

ISBN: 978-1-950305-60-5 (sc)
ISBN: 978-1-950305-61-2 (ebook)

First printing edition: February 26, 2021
Published by JournalStone Publishing in the United States of America.
Cover Design: Trevor Henderson | Cover Layout: Sophy Romvari
Edited by Sean Leonard
Proofreading and Interior Layout by Scarlett R. Algee

JournalStone Publishing
3205 Sassafras Trail
Carbondale, Illinois 62901

JournalStone books may be ordered through booksellers or by contacting:
JournalStone | www.journalstone.com

To all the good teachers.

Shelter
for the
DAMNED

SUBURBAN SOMEWHERE
2003

Chapter 1

MARK SAW THE OUTLINE OF SOMETHING etched against the moon, something vaguely house-shaped. He stopped.

Adam, whose eyes were cast down under his hood, failed to react in time and thudded into Mark's back.

"What the shit, Mark?" He rubbed the corner of his skull that had bonked Mark's sharp shoulder blade and followed his friend's eyeline. "What is that?"

Scott, who'd been trailing further behind, said, "It's a house."

The boys drew nearer. Shadowy details revealed themselves slowly.

"It's too small to be a house," Adam said.

"It's shaped like a house," Scott said.

Adam spat an arc of saliva, shoved his fists into the pockets of his jeans. "More like a shed."

Scott shook his head. "It's shaped like a house."

"People fuckin' live in houses," Adam said.

"Maybe somebody used to live in there."

"When?"

"I don't know."

Adam laughed. "Mark, will you talk some goddamn sense into this fool? I mean, let me just throw this out there—what kind of a wussy tucks his T-shirt into his jeans, for Christ's sake? What is this, the nineteen-fuckin-fifties?"

Adam had hit a familiar sore spot. Not only did Scott's dad force him to tuck in his shirts, he also forced him to *iron* his shirts, and even his jeans. Mark wouldn't be surprised to learn that he was made to polish his sneakers, too.

Scott hissed something nasty between bared teeth and yanked his oversized T-shirt from the waist of his pants.

Adam scoffed.

Mark had been half-listening to his friends, but he said nothing. Adam paced and readjusted his hood. He shot a glance at Scott that said, *Stop being such a baby.*

Scott flattened his shirt with the palms of his hands, then stood still. He tried to look aloof, but looked scared shitless instead.

Mark continued staring at the place, all frayed splinters of wood and flat, desiccated walls. He could almost feel its texture, simply by looking at it.

"Who the fuck would live in there?" Adam directed the question at no one in particular.

It looked impossibly weathered, transformed by age. Mark couldn't help but notice that, by some unexplainable stroke of luck or happenstance, it was untouched by late-night prowlers and graffiti artists. It wore no evidence of vandalism, no etchings or street tags.

"Nobody lives in there." Mark's response slipped out with all the grace of bad slapstick comedy; it might've been the first thing he'd said all evening. It wasn't difficult to remain silent when he was with Adam and Scott. He allowed Adam to shout his opinions and he allowed Scott to fervently disagree with said opinions.

Adam wiped his bangs out of his eyes. "So we can smoke in there."

Mark didn't even take a moment to pause. "Do you have cigarettes?"

"Courtesy of my big brother."

Scott stepped forward and held out his hands. "Hold on, guys. Come on, we can't smoke in somebody's house. Be smart. They'll call the cops."

"Who'll call the cops, Scott?" Adam said. "Think about it."

"The people inside the house, that's who." Then, after a pause, he nodded at Adam's Alice Cooper pullover hoodie. "And who the hell wears rock band merch anymore?"

Adam ignored the weak, belated comeback and gazed heavenward, as if imploring God to knock some sense into his paranoid buddy. "It's not a house, for Christ's sake."

"What is it, then?" Scott said.

"It's a shack," Mark said. Yeah, that seemed right.

"A shack?" Scott echoed. "People live in shacks. Come on. Let's go somewhere else."

"It's dark out here," Adam said, an unlit cigarette wagging from the side of his mouth. "Nobody's going to see us. Besides, it'll be safer in there than it is out here. If somebody sees us smoking out here and makes the right call, my dad will peel my skull like a fuckin' orange. I'm going in."

Scott turned to Mark. "What do you think?"

Mark looked hard at the shack. It had the symmetry and structure of any beat-up old building, like a tool shed you might find in some forgotten industrial place—but there was something formless about it. The walls looked sewn together, like an invisible force was holding them upright. He sniffed at the chilly night air. He stared off into the field's surrounding area, where boxy houses of privatized comfort were separated by equally distanced lawns. Those houses had people living inside of them. The houses had names and addresses and porch lights and *Welcome Home* mats on their doorsteps. By contrast, the shack defied shape. It defied color. It was an assortment of nondescript grays.

There was definitely *something* about it. How had they never seen it before? Mark was sure they had crossed this very field at least once, if not several times, and yet they had never taken notice of it. His brain was blaring with strange excitement. *Go on, take a chance.*

"I'm going in, too," he said, keeping his voice level.

He set his eyes on a fissure between the door and the wall. A distant slit, a hair's worth of blackness. A teasing glimpse of inside.

Adam nodded, slipped a cigarette to Mark, then held the pack out to Scott. "You coming with us or what?"

Scott fixed his eyes on the shack. Bobbed uncertainly on his feet. Mark thought he saw him shudder.

"Shit, come on, Scott," Adam said. "Don't throw a big fuss over it."

Scott yanked a cigarette from the pack. "Fine, let's go already."

"Now that's what I'm talking about," Adam said.

They approached the shack, clutching smokes inside their fists. Mark reached the door first. As he stepped toward it, something like a gust of heat sighed from inside, breathed into his skin, massaged his muscles and coiled his bones. Damn, it was getting cold outside.

There was no doorknob. Nor was there a hole where a doorknob might have been. The entrance was a flush, unbroken surface. Mark eased his fingers into the crack between the door and the wall, and warmth gushed out again, subtler now. He pulled a little and the door crunched open.

"Why don't we try someplace else, guys?" Scott said.

Adam jumped on the spot, like a cartoon character having a tantrum. "Fuckin' give it a rest, Scott, will you?"

Scott grabbed Mark's shoulder and restrained Adam with his other arm. "Hold on for one second. What if somebody's in there? This is a breaking and entering sort of situation."

"Will you for Christ's sake look at the place, man?" Adam said. "It's fucking ancient."

"Don't yell at me," Scott said.

"I'm not yelling. I'm trying to make a for Christ's sake point."

"You're yelling your point."

Unlike Adam, Scott had something to lose. Scott's parents were diligent, merciless monitors; if he did anything wrong, they'd know within minutes. Somehow, they always did. Adam, on the other hand, faced the daily possibility of getting yelled at or whacked, regardless of what he did.

"Adam, relax," Mark said. "Scott, listen to me. Nobody could live in this place. Look at the size of it. We're in the middle of the suburbs. Who would live in some shack in the middle of a field? There are nice houses everywhere. Think about it."

"Okay, then why is it here?" Scott insisted.

Mark quickly discovered that he couldn't muster an answer. "I don't know," he said. "So we can have a place to smoke."

Scott didn't return Mark's smirk, but he looked calmer for a moment, before a somber expression crossed his face. "What if somebody died in there?"

"Nobody died in there," Mark said. "Nobody lived in there."

"If somebody died in there, we would know about it by now," Adam said. "Everyone goes crazy over haunted houses and shit like that."

Scott tilted his head to the side. "I don't know…"

"Okay, what don't you know? We've outlined this whole situation pretty clearly," Adam said.

"I just don't know if it's a good idea…"

"For fuck's sake."

"Adam, please be quiet," Mark said. "Look, Scott, you want to smoke a cigarette, right?" If nothing else, he could always appeal to Scott's intensifying nicotine cravings.

"Sure," Scott said.

"Okay," Mark said, "let's weigh out the pros and cons: if somebody's in there, and I really don't think anybody is, we can just say we had no clue that we weren't allowed inside."

Scott opened his mouth to speak, hesitated, then shot his hands into the air—an *I give up* gesture. "Okay, fine. Jesus, you're insistent, the both of you."

"Fucking finally," Adam said.

"Go to hell," Scott said.

Mark entered first. The outside suburban air bled into the shack's interior. It was warmer and drier in the shack, yes, but he felt something much more specific than that, much less physical. There was a transition. Mark paused, allowing it to set in.

The walls of the shack looked like they'd been painted with shadows. The windows were coated in grime. The place had two levels, the top even darker than the bottom. Tendrils of moonlight snaked through the rot, exposing detail. Everything was made of wood; everything was gray. It looked as if no one had been in here for decades.

The three boys' sets of eyes drifted to the staircase. Scott and Adam took a mutually indifferent glance, but Mark's eyes lingered. His gaze crawled up the incline and he squinted, trying to distinguish forms in the darkness. He took a step forward and craned his neck in an effort to see more detail.

Adam's voice broke his focus. "What are you doing?"

Mark turned, dazed. A wan smile pulled his lips.

He couldn't explain exactly what he felt in that moment. Sort of an ebbing…like he'd just been caught up in the best film he'd ever seen, and for a few seconds had actually forgotten about the world outside the screen. He stopped replaying recent arguments with Mom and Dad, lost any concerns about his slipping grades, about the often creeping sense that all the authority figures were right, that there was *something wrong* with him. As soon as he entered, he didn't want to leave. He was not equipped to understand. He only knew that, in this strange and intense moment, he wanted to breathe the shack's squalid air forever.

Adam approached him and flicked his lighter to life. The flame coloured the murk with a marble of orange light. Mark dipped his cigarette, sucking filter and then smoke. The tobacco tasted good, and the nicotine rush was even better, but he wasn't concerned with those things.

Right now, nothing mattered but the place itself.

The Shack.

Adam and Scott lit their cigarettes and sat cross-legged on the floor.

"Okay, I admit it," Scott said. "This place is kind of interesting. I wonder what it is."

Gray smoke trailed from Adam's nostrils. "It's Satan's pad. It's a spaceship. It's a monster's stomach. Who gives a shit? It's a place to enjoy a fucking cigarette."

Mark's body came alive, tingling as he approached his friends. He sat beside them, pulling smoke into his throat.

"You see?" Adam continued. "Nobody's jumping out to kill us. No fuckin' ghosts. No crazy shit."

Scott tapped ashes onto the floor. "You wouldn't know if there were ghosts in here."

"What are you talking about?" Adam said.

"Ghosts are invisible," Scott replied.

"How do you know? Have you ever seen one?"

"No," Scott said. "They're invisible, idiot."

"Fuck off."

They sat for hours, talking dirty in the rot and gloom. Mark had never taken so long to smoke a cigarette. He half-listened, but mostly he just breathed. Mostly he just felt.

Chapter 2

"WHOA," MARK SAID. "WHAT THE FUCK?"

Clinton huffed and gasped. "What the hell'd ya just say ta me?"

"Calm the fuck…" Mark was cut off as he ducked and dodged. "Whoa."

"What'd ya say ta me?"

The scuffle between Mark and Clinton must've started with something Mark had said, or maybe with the gestures he'd made while speaking.

A forgotten source (a therapist? a teacher?) had once told Mark that ninety percent of human communication was conveyed through body language. Or maybe it was seventy-eight percent, or eighty-three. The undetermined figure might've been delivered to him in last year's mandatory Preparing for Life class, accompanied by a blue and red pie chart: Blue as Body Language, Red as Everything Else. Red, the words one chooses to use, the volume of one's voice, and other factors now unknown to Mark.

Mark had been standing in the school field with his friends, unseen by lunchtime supervisors, when Clinton shuffled past, huge and forlorn, tugging a piece of beef jerky with his teeth. That was when Mark had said whatever it was that set this chaos into motion.

Did it have something to do with the jerky? Probably not, but it was a possibility. Could a remark about a lunchtime snack spark a violent altercation? Mark had seen fights start over less. He had started fights over less.

Much, much less.

Although he'd spoken only moments ago, he couldn't remember what he'd said any more clearly than he could remember the communicatory percentage assigned to Body Language.

He had spaced out, something he found himself doing more and more often these past few weeks, it seemed, and he'd said just the right thing or, depending on one's perspective, just the wrong thing.

Clinton stopped and spun, a single rippling motion, and he faced Mark, dropping tattered jerky by his side.

Scott and Adam stepped back at once.

"You picked your battle, man," Adam said.

Clinton's angry blinders went up. Mark had seen this happen many times to many people, and it always meant violence. Hard, fast, thoughtless violence.

Mark's palms dampened. His face warmed. Tense shakes vibrated under, through, and over his skin; these feelings were familiar—the physical symptoms of prefight preparation.

Clinton swung a fist that looked, to Mark, about the size of a ripe honeydew melon. Mark heard the splitting of air, slivers away from his face. He knew right away that he couldn't take this giant kid for long. Clinton was skipping the obligatory hissing and hair-raising and getting right down to face-crushing business.

"Come on, you guys, back me up," Mark said.

"No way," Adam said.

Mark turned, an attempt to will Scott and Adam from inaction, but he could only spare a brief and hostile glimpse. Right now he had to worry about Clinton, who after failing to land his first punch, was taking a moment to marinate in rapidly mounting rage.

The moment was brief.

Clinton burst, a whirling monsoon of flesh. Saliva frothed his lips and cheeks. His wet hair flapped, speckling his forehead with a cocktail of sweat and spit. He sprayed drool and threats and fists that missed, for the most part, until, after minutes of frenzied swiping, he finally landed a hit.

And it was a motherfucker of a hit.

A square of knuckles smashed Mark's chest, sent a tremor rattling through his body. His skull jostled, his jaws clamped, an incisor cut his tongue. Another punch connected with his temple and he rocked on his feet. His ears sang with the sound of something fractured. Next, Clinton's fist mashed his lips, but he was still standing. Breathing in wheezes. Mouth swishing with the coppery flavour of blood.

He wished like hell that he was in the Shack again.

He dropped back as Clinton took another arcing swing, then sprawled on the grass, painting his ass green. He scuttled away, but Clinton didn't advance.

No, Clinton didn't advance at all. He just hovered over Mark, arms raised. Western stance, reaching for invisible pistols. He looked down, his enormous head eclipsing the sun.

Mark would've been terrified if not for Clinton's expression.

Mark watched it happen; Clinton breaking through the surface of rage. A sort of baptism that left the big galoot gasping and humiliated on the other side—and his face wasn't only wet with saliva; no, it was wet with tears, too. Mark had seen lots of guys cry after a fight, but never in the middle of one.

Clinton looked at him for a long time, breathing in ragged bursts.

"Fuck you," Mark said.

Clinton raised a hammy arm, reconsidered, and muttered something half-tough before moving away, his head looking somehow loose on his neck, drooping down to stare at his own soaked shirt-front.

The fight, or one-sided ass kicking, to be more accurate, ended so quickly that Mark couldn't summon a response. He sat up and stared at a random point in space. Disbelief. His heart thudded against a sternum that felt shattered.

Scott and Adam finally shuffled up behind him. Scott reached down to help him up, but Mark yanked away.

"The hell didn't you guys back me up?" He stood up and spat a red glob. He wiped his hand across his lips. Stuck a finger in his mouth to make sure everything was still intact. "Feels like I cut my tongue in half."

"You fuckin' deserved it," Adam said.

"For what?" Mark asked. "For making a fucking joke? Have you seen the size of that kid?"

"Man, you started it."

"I did what? Made a joke. Everybody makes jokes. Not everybody gets their face split open over it."

Truthfully, Mark still couldn't recall whether it had even been a joke that had sparked this particular brawl. Based on his wide-ranging record of fistfights, though, he thought it fair to assume he'd said the wrong thing at the wrong time. Again.

Scott cast his eyes down. Real contemplative. Mark wanted to slap him upside the head.

"His dad just died," Scott said.

Mark brushed grass from his knees with scuffed palms. "Whose dad? Clinton's dad? Are you serious?"

"Heart attack," Scott said.

Mark bobbed on the balls of his feet. Shaking off the shakes. "How old was he?"

"I don't know," Scott said. "Our parents' age."

Mark stopped moving. "Shit. Really?"

"Yes, really, so watch your mouth," Adam said. "You're stupid sometimes, Mark."

Blood leaked out the side of Mark's mouth and scrawled a rivulet down his chin. He watched Clinton's slow shuffle across the field; the kid had just finished knocking Mark's brains around and now he was throwing a one-man pity party. Mark wanted to tell Adam to go fuck himself, and he was a breath away from doing so until he got a good look at Adam's face. Adam looked no more willing to be fucked with than Clinton had looked just a minute ago. Mark was all too familiar with the expression that Adam wore. He had seen it a few times, most of them memorable.

In a bad way.

He didn't need to reach too far back into his memory to remember where he'd gotten the scar on the back of his shoulder. It had all started with a walk to the corner store near Adam's house, on a mission to buy cigarettes. It was the only place they'd found where they could buy smokes, since none of them was even close to passing for eighteen. The owner of the store, an oil-haired twentysomething named Brett, was willing to supply them with the goods on three conditions: one, that they paid a twenty percent markup; two, that they waited until nobody else was in the store before making their purchase; and three, that they told nobody else about the arrangement. Truth be told, Mark resented paying sixteen dollars for a pack of cigarettes, but it was a compromise he was grudgingly willing to make.

They always took the same route to the store. When they arrived, they would wait if necessary, and then they'd chain-smoke their way back to Adam's place. It was a tradition both menial and colossal, a routine linked with the freewheeling heat of summer.

On one eventful walk to the store, Mark had given in to the urge to start some shit. He'd picked up a dirt-crusted bottle from the side of the road and begun tossing it between his hands. He'd noticed Scott's neatly pressed shirt, Sunday school clean, and he'd been unable to resist: he'd shaken the bottle at Scott, spraying some brownish liquid on his collar. Scott frantically wiped it off and told Mark to stop screwing around.

Mark laughed and shook the bottle again.

Scott got really pissed and, jogging backwards, said, "I mean it, stop fucking around."

Mark still advanced, a laugh-staggered sprint, holding the bottle like a magnum. Scott stopped and shoved him to the ground, where he lay for a few seconds, still cradling the grimy bottle.

Adam and Scott kept walking. Mark watched them.

Adam looked indifferent to the situation, but Scott hissed, "I wish he would just learn when not to screw around."

Mark looked—no, *stared*, almost pensively, at the bottle. Smirked for nobody but himself, then threw the thing as hard as he could.

If there was anything he'd learned from his countless sports team failures, it was that he couldn't throw for shit. The bottle, unsurprisingly, didn't make it far, but its landing made a statement. It took a few somersaults in the air, then dove inches to the left of Adam and Scott.

There was a pop as it connected with the summer-fried pavement. Glass sprayed the sidewalk and clinked all over the road.

Scott wheeled around. "Seriously, what the hell is wrong with you?"

"Don't shove me," Mark said.

A car squeal-stopped by the sidewalk as Mark and Scott advanced on each other. The door opened and slammed shut, an angry adult sound. Mark turned. A middle-aged man, whose youth was melting beneath a too-tight polo shirt, stomped toward them, his teeth clenched, his sunglasses glinting. His comb-over bobbed as he moved.

"Okay, who's the smartass?" the man said.

Adam, who'd maintained his cool throughout the ordeal, pointed at Mark.

The man said nothing before marching toward Mark with drill sergeant intensity. He pinched his sunglasses with both hands and yanked them off. Playing Clint Eastwood. Playing Angry Daddy. Playing God.

"You wanna pop someone's tires, you little shit?" the man asked. "You wanna cause an accident? Huh? Think you're funny?"

Mark heard a strain in the man's tone; this guy wasn't Mark's dad or Adam's dad. No, this guy had next to no potential for active violence in his blood. He wasn't the tough guy he believed himself to be; this was not his genuine state. He was a jaded suburbanite company man, Mark decided, who was re-enacting one of many scenes from channel 45's eternally looping Cop Cinema Classics marathon.

"I didn't mean to throw it," Mark said. A thin, facetious smile wormed through his composure.

This could get interesting; although this guy might've only perceived himself as a man among hardnosed men, he was also the kind of angry that causes lawsuits.

"You accidentally threw a bottle right in front of my car?" the man asked.

Mark maintained eye contact. That was the thing with these kinds of dogs. You had to know when to recognize and when to acknowledge, but you also had to know when to dispense with the bait.

"I threw it on the sidewalk," Mark said.

"But you still threw it, wiseass."

"It flew out of my hands."

There was a period of silence. The temporal equivalent of two consecutive sneezes. The man looked at the boys and twisted his sunglasses between thumb and forefinger, his eyes narrowed into *don't fuck with me* slits. Tom Selleck meets Tom Cruise. The badass of the 'burbs.

"I'm gonna remember all three of you," he said. "Don't come around here again or I'll call the cops. Especially you, tough guy. Hear me, you little shit?"

Mark sustained his stare.

Action Hero speed-walked back to his car. He dropped in, slammed the door, and peeled off, leaving a Firestone smudge on the road.

Real cinematic.

Mark turned to Adam. "What's your problem? Scott starts shit and you rat me out? Fuck you, Adam."

Adam had appeared completely aloof until this moment. Now, the look he fixed on Mark seemed almost like an impersonation of their Comb-over Crusader. In fact, Mark probably would've laughed if Adam hadn't looked so downright, authentically, unmistakably furious. He shoved Mark.

Mark lost his footing, but quickly jumped back up. "What's your problem?"

Adam gave him another shove, more forceful this time. Wind whooshed from Mark's lungs as he thudded against a fence. A wood splinter sliced his shoulder. Adam lunged, forearm outstretched, and restrained him against it. The splinter cut deeper.

Pain like a drawn-out papercut.

"I know who that guy is," Adam said. "He plays cards with my dad sometimes. If he comes to my fucking house, I'm not going to take shit for this."

Mark tried to move away from the fence, away from the puncturing strip of wood, but Adam continued pressing. The splinter pierced and split Mark's skin, drawing blood. Adam pushed more forcefully. The splinter probed deeper into Mark's flesh, and he couldn't help but shout in shock at the white-hot pain.

"Christ, Adam, let go of me!"

Adam drew his forearm away, hesitant, deliberate, and Mark swore quietly. He dabbed his bleeding shoulder and, not knowing what else to say, grumbled, "He obviously didn't recognize you."

"That's not the fuckin' point," Adam said.

"What is the point, then?"

No answer. Adam was already far ahead.

Adam refused to return to the convenience store after that day. Mark still had a pink exclamation point of a scar from the splinter in the fence.

Adam could be violent the way most people can blink.

The bell rang and, for a moment, Mark stood in head-throbbing disorientation, lost in the double-memory of split-second lapses from calmness to violence.

He looked down at himself. He was splattered with bloodstains and grass stains and sweat. He brushed his hand across his chin and saw that his palm was wet with redness.

Adam turned and began walking back toward the school, Scott trailing close behind. "Come on, man. We're going to be late for class."

Mark followed them. "Clinton must've mutilated my mouth. It won't stop bleeding."

"Yeah, he hit you pretty good," Scott said.

"He didn't have to *hit him good*, Scott," Adam said. "The kid's a fuckin' giant."

"He landed the hits right," Scott said. "If he had only clipped Mark, this wouldn't have happened. No, that cat's got technique."

"It doesn't fucking matter," Adam said. "Clinton is a titan."

Mark wiped his filthy palms on his filthier jeans. "I'm going to need to clean myself up. I don't want to show up to Ms. Corr's class looking like this."

Ms. Corr, the concerned parent type, thought rough teenagers still swore in *damns* and *hells*, thought they played softball and drank soda pop for thrills, thought Mark was a serious problem child, a real live specimen of the violent delinquent type because he'd been to the office twelve too many times for her liking. Mark wasn't like the rest of the kids, not if you asked Ms. Corr. To her mind, he needed correction. He needed reprogramming.

Adam, Scott, and Mark entered the school in a tightly packed line, navigating through the bustle and chatter of crowds.

Mark crossed the hall toward the washroom. "See you guys in a bit, all right?"

"Yeah, all right," Scott said, disappearing behind Adam, always behind Adam, into the undulating body of bodies.

Mark pushed the washroom door with hesitation. He was relieved to see that there were no muscleheads or stoners around to ask him, "Hey, bro, what the blue fuck happened to you?" The room was empty, humming with the kind of drip-drop, fuzzy white silence saved especially for public restrooms.

Mark walked to the sink and inspected his face in the mirror. He wasn't visibly bruised, but he could feel his mouth refilling with blood. He spat a heavy, crimson wad down the drain and gargled metallic school-water.

He glanced again at the mirror. His reflected features were divided by a thick black epithet that someone had scrawled on the mirror.

I should've taken a swing at Clinton, he thought.

His T-shirt had been stretched out of shape by Clinton's fat, swiping hands. The wide collar exposed his bones, and anybody could see now that he was unnaturally skinny. Weird skinny. Scary skinny. *Hey, kid, what's wrong with you, don't your parents feed you* skinny.

He wiped the blood away. Splashed water to clean the dried stuff. Grimaced at his acne-speckled face. The poke of his bones, the bulge of his eyes. His buzz-saw haircut. He always felt uneasy in the presence of his own reflection. Like he was sharing silence with a hologram. He rushed out of the bathroom, eyes averted from the mirror.

He practically jogged through the halls to get to Ms. Corr's math class, slowing only when a square-jawed gym teacher barked at him, "Hey, hotshot, put the brakes on."

Despite his best efforts, he arrived late. He gingerly opened the door, attracting a few half-conscious stares from his classmates.

Ms. Corr, writing on the blackboard, paused mid-numeral. "Thanks for coming."

"Yeah. Sorry," Mark said, slouching into his desk.

Madeline Fraley, sitting in front of him, gave a nonplussed glance in his direction. He smiled at her.

She smiled back, as she always did. He never missed Ms. Corr's class, and the main reason was because of Madeline's smile. He'd never spoken to Madeline, but she always smiled. Maybe they would never speak, and maybe Mark never wanted to speak.

Maybe he just wanted a stranger's smile.

After class, Mark and Adam walked with Scott toward his locker.

"Between us three," Mark said, "I love the way Madeline smiles."

"Why don't you just fuckin' bone her already?" Adam asked.

"Adam, come on. That's not what I'm talking about."

"And I'm not a fuckin' living breathing organism."

"Huh?" Scott said.

"It means Mark's full of shit, for Christ's sake."

"Oh."

Mark had developed a fascination with Madeline's personal history, as disclosed by snippets of conversations he'd eavesdropped. He'd once heard that she snuck a bottle of Beefeater into a school dance, hiding the bottle under a loose floorboard in the gymnasium. She'd finished most of the bottle herself, taking undiluted swigs in cones of darkness untouched by strobe and disco light. She'd found some lucky but unnamed stranger when the dance had finished, the gender of whom was frequently debated, and she'd brought said stranger home with her. Darker rumours, quiet whisper-rumours disclosed in the illusion of secrecy, suggested that Madeline never wore skirts or shorts, even in the hottest of summer months, for definitively unspoken reasons. She heated paper clips and sewing needles with a Bic lighter, the rumours stated, and burned star-shaped scars into the flesh of her thighs. These were details that Mark kept from Scott and Adam, who would probably ask him how the hell he'd gathered all this information without ever actually speaking with her.

What Mark *did* talk about was how pretty he thought she was. Studded bracelets and belts, long hair always tied back, an angular face and eyes that could make anyone look down at their shoes. She carried herself like someone much older. If Mark ever spoke with her, he knew, she'd be the person to tell him what was what.

The three friends paused by Scott's locker and Scott proceeded to fumble aggressively with his lock. Kicking and clanging and cursing. He'd forgotten his lock combination, as always. He gave Mark a pleading look, as always. Like Mark was supposed to know his combo.

Mark ignored him.

As always.

"It's Friday," Mark said. "We should do something. You know, this weekend, tonight, whatever."

"Yeah, all right," Adam said. "Any plans?"

"Do you want to go to the Shack? Just an idea," Mark replied.

The way Mark saw it, they didn't even need to smoke in order to get something out of that space. The real rush was the Shack itself. Not that he could ever expect his friends to understand. It'd been months since they'd last been there.

Scott finally recalled his combo and opened his locker. "I don't know. My dad keeps saying he wants me to help out around the house."

Mark watched him pull a stack of textbooks from the top of his locker. "So what? Just make sure you're home early. Help out tomorrow morning."

Scott stared placidly in response. Flattened his combed hair with the palm of his hand. Boy scout clean.

"Fine, if you're scared, we can go alone." He turned to Adam. "You up for it?"

Adam shrugged. "I don't know, man. I'm not feeling it tonight."

"Why not?" Mark asked.

Scott glanced at a nearby clock and muttered something about running late. A distracted science teacher bumped into Adam. The man's glasses bounced off to clatter and spin across the floor. He picked them up, mumbled, and continued huffing down the hallway. Adam stared after him.

"Why not?" Mark repeated, louder this time.

"I don't know," Adam said. "Not feeling it."

"What do you mean, *not feeling it*?" Mark said. "What's with you two today?"

Adam leaned against a locker and stretched his fingers behind his neck. "I just don't see the point of going there anymore. Sure, it was fun the first couple of times, but I just think it's fucking stupid now."

"Stupid? Why is it stupid?" Mark said.

"Because. It's just stupid. Why would I sit in a fuckin' shack when I can drink or smoke or get laid, for Christ's sake? And besides, it's getting a bit risky."

"*Get laid*, he says. As if. Neither of you creeps has ever had a girlfriend," Mark said bluntly.

Adam ignored him. "I said it's fucking risky, okay? Give it a rest."

"Risky how? What's the problem? I feel like I'm talking to Scott right now," Mark said.

"Go to hell," Scott said, without looking at him.

"Maybe I just don't want to go, man," Adam said.

"You're not even giving me a reason," Mark said. "Jesus, the least you can do is give me a reason."

"Mark, honestly, I just don't want to fuckin' go. If you want to do something different, I'm up for ideas."

Mark sucked his lower lip and tried to look calm. In reality, he was restraining a scream of fury. He wanted a little bit of that warm, indescribable sensation again; whatever it was that had snuck inside his skull to hug his stress-rattled brain, it was something he could use more of.

"You guys are making no sense right now," he said. "You sound like slaves to your daddies, that's what I think."

"Ooh," Scott said quietly, avoiding his eyes.

Adam wouldn't look away. No, he glared right back. Mark's post-fight rage was still coursing dully through his body, threatening to push back out. Adam's eyes, which had every bit as much rage in them as Mark's, were the reason Mark kept his true feelings at bay.

After a moment, the school bell broke their silence. They took the cue and broke the uncomfortable tableau to walk down the hall. Adam and Scott began debating over contenders for the most attractive girl in their math class, and Mark listened with utter disinterest.

He decided not to bother bringing up the Shack again.

For now.

Chapter 3

MARK SLOUCHED IN HIS SEAT AT the back of the bus, his chest aching dimly. Staring out the window, he traced the route, half-thoughts drifting through his afternoon-dumb mind. The sound of the motor lulled him into a dim and daydreamy state, softening the edge of his waning adrenaline.

Evenly spaced houses flicked by in a calm and stately procession of cream, russet, taupe, Tarrytown green. Mark imagined the Shack planted between two of those soft-hued homes. He envisioned the scenario in detail, a colorless and skeletal imposition among burgundy and navy idyll, shadows cast across carefully maintained rooftops. He imagined the Shack closer to the cozy abodes—on Mr. and Mrs. Suburbanite's driveway, beside a child's basketball hoop, or maybe perched in the middle of some well-to-do couple's lawn. He imagined frantic phone calls to the police, to the city council, to the People in Authority. He imagined hypothetical scenarios as elaborate mind-movies: tight-lipped women and men with hands on belted hips, gathering around the Shack, murmuring to each other about the threat of serial killers, of the homeless, of anarchists.

He nearly missed his stop, hypnotized, an open-eyed dream state. He pulled the Next Stop cord on the cusp of a shift between bus benches, moments before the right stop would've slipped out of reach, opening space for the wrong one instead. He stepped off the bus and walked the path, unconsciously engrained, that led to his house. He nodded to a crimson-faced woman who held a tangle of weeds in her dirt-trailing hand. She wiped her sweaty brow with the back of a wrist and said "hello," almost inaudibly, her eyes phantasmal, her features gaunt.

As Mark approached his house, he saw Dad's Subaru reflecting sunlight in the driveway. Mom's Subaru was not parked beside it yet.

Dad was mowing the lawn, his eyebrows bunched in focus over a pair of sunglasses. His vast bald head gleamed in the sunlight. Muscles bunched inside his enormous shoulders. Mark walked past him toward the front door.

Dad waved. Yelled something over the buzzing din of the motor. Mark waved back and gave thumbs up, pretending like he heard, and walked inside.

Mark couldn't tell if Dad was happy or angry, even despite the friendly wave. Sunglasses always masked Dad's mood. Like tinted ciphers.

Mark thought that maybe Dad knew about the fight with Clinton, either by Mark's expression or by a bloodspot that he had forgotten to wash off. Adrenaline crept back into his system, slowly. Like poison.

The first time Dad had found out about one of Mark's fights, he'd forced Mark to stand facing the mirrored door of the front hall closet. Dad had stood behind him, looking bigger than a father ought to look.

"So, what? Do you think it's cool to get in fights?" Dad had asked.

"No, I don't think it's cool," Mark had answered.

"What, then? You think it makes you look tough?"

"No."

"That's not what the principal was telling me. I want you to show me how tough you are."

"I'm not tough," Mark said. "I don't think I'm tough."

"That's not what the school principal was telling me today."

"I know that fighting is stupid. I won't do it again."

"Come on," Dad said. "Show me how tough you are."

Mark stared into the mirror and reflected eye contact. Dad looked totally and utterly removed.

"Don't wait for Mom to come home," Dad said. "I see what you're thinking. Show me."

"I don't know what you want me to do."

"Look at your reflection and say all the things that you said to that kid today," Dad said.

"I don't think I said anything," Mark said.

"You're lying to me."

"I didn't say anything. It didn't happen that way. It just…it happened. He bumped my shoulder and I pushed him and then we had a fight."

"Okay, show me," Dad said.

"Show you what?" Mark asked.

"Show me how you fought."

"We just fought. It just happened."

"So show me."

Mark trembled. He gave reflection Dad a pleading look. He couldn't turn around and really look him in the eyes. No, there was no way he could do that.

"Dad…"

"Show me," Dad said. "Show me and you can go."

Mark gave a few swings, self-conscious, harm-conscious. Body quaking. Dad had never hit him before, not exactly, but he had definitely gotten physical. At the age of six or seven, Mark had wedged a peanut butter sandwich into the VCR. Simple as that: he'd clogged the machinery, rendering it gooey and useless. When Dad asked him about it, Mark said he didn't know how it got there. Dad grabbed him by the front of his shirt, hard enough to stretch it out of shape, then lifted him into the air, where his suspended feet swayed and clacked together. "Don't insult my intelligence," Dad had said again and again, quietly, through gritted teeth, right in Mark's scared shitless little face, until he finally admitted what he'd done. Then Dad lowered him to the floor and gave him a hug.

Dad snorted after Mark mock-fought his own reflection. "Look how ridiculous. Do you see how ridiculous you are? I'm going to fill you in on something. You're not as tough as you think."

Chapter 4

MARK TOOK A PIECE OF SALAMI from the fridge, rolled it into a ball, and wedged it in his mouth. He swished Pepsi, spat carbonated blood into the sink, then jogged up the stairs to his room, where he dropped his backpack on the heat register and flopped onto his bed.

He was only there for a moment before Dad came inside.

"How was your day?" Dad called from the kitchen.

"Good," Mark called back.

"Come downstairs and talk to me. I don't have the money for a long-distance call."

One of Dad's old jokes.

Mark walked down and saw Dad's sunglasses on the counter. Dad was crouched over the sink, his big back bobbing as he sucked water from the faucet. He paused and looked over his shoulder, half-panting. He switched off the tap and turned around. Clapped together his hands, like he was ready to run a drill. "So. How was your day?" Sweat beaded his forehead and glued his shirt to his chest. Dad always looked happy after mowing the lawn, the way some might look after scoring the game's winning goal, or in the midst of opening a particularly thoughtful gift. He always said he liked to see the lawn go from ugly to pretty. Said it with a half-cocked smile, like everybody else was in on the feeling, too.

"It was okay," Mark said. "I'm glad it's the weekend."

"Yeah, me too," Dad said. "This weather. This weather is exceptional. Would you agree with that, Mark? *Exceptional?* You know what else is exceptional? That lawn, my man. Not one blade too long. The thing was ugly, but now it's pretty."

He chuckled. Mark smiled. A chickadee sang outside the window.

"What's for dinner?" Mark asked.

Dad was bent over the sink again, halfway through another gulp of water. He raised his index finger, a silent *wait a minute* gesture. He whirled around and gasped, like he'd been swimming in the stuff rather than drinking it. "I don't know yet. I'm considering Chinese food again, from that new place. Chong's or Wong's or whatever the name…but your mother might be getting tired of it. I think I'm becoming a fiend for the take-out Chinese food lately. Or maybe it's just Chong's I'm fiending for. The other night Mom says to me, *Honey, we can't just order in every night.* I said we don't order every night, but then I thought about it… I guess I ordered pizza on Tuesday, and Mom was out on Wednesday, so I called our trusty Wong's, and we ate the leftovers on Thursday." He laughed in disbelief. "Like I'm a bachelor again. Let's see what I can do when she gets home."

It didn't matter much to Mark what they would be eating. He consumed food as fuel, almost completely indifferent to its forms and variations. Still, he smiled like he was on Dad's side. Like he was on Team Take-Out.

"So how are your classes going?" Dad asked. "Are you beginning to get the hang of that math class you're taking?"

"I don't know. It's pretty difficult," Mark said.

"Yeah, well…so was abolishing slavery."

Mark scoffed.

Dad made a boxer's pose. "What, you think I'm being culturally insensitive, huh? Want to pick a fight over it?"

Mark faked a laugh. "Sorry."

Dad peeled off his shirt and used it to dab his sweating armpits. "Don't be sorry. I'm just joking with you, my man. For real, though, I know you say the word *difficult*, but I don't want to see any F's on that report card."

"I won't fail," Mark said.

Dad gave Mark an exasperated look and squeezed his shoulder. "I know you're not going to fail…but let's take preventative measures, right? If you're still having a hard time, I'm sure the teacher would be happy to lend a helping hand."

"I'll catch on," Mark said.

Dad opened the dishwasher. Hot white steam billowed into his face and he drew back, emitting a theatrical cough. He looked at Mark through squinted eyes. "So what kind of stuff are you guys learning in that social studies class? You're taking that right now, yeah?"

"Yeah," Mark said. In the background of his mind, he remembered having this very same conversation less than a week ago.

He decided not to mention it.

"I used to love that class. They used to call it history. They *do* call it social studies now, right?" Dad asked, carrying a high stack of plates from the dishwasher to the cupboard. "You want to give me a hand with these?"

"Yeah."

Mark picked up a bundle of forks, still hot from the steam. He rushed to the utensil drawer and dropped them with a clatter.

"Careful, Mark," Dad said. "Jesus Louiseus, my man."

"Sorry."

"It's all right, just don't go burning yourself. What kind of stuff are you learning in social studies?"

"I don't know," Mark said. "Mostly history."

"Yeah, that's what they used to call it, history."

"Yeah."

"I hope they teach you guys something about this country. The way things really are." Dad shook his head. "Things are in a crunch. You guys are all going to have to learn how to save your money." He juggled six glasses to the cupboard with red starfish hands.

"Maybe they'll get into it later," Mark said.

"I hope so. The way things are going at work lately. This new guy's on my ass like the whole company's going to fall apart tomorrow. And who the hell knows, right?" He stared into space, coffee cups squeezed between his forearms and biceps. "'Who the hell knows?' You can say that again."

Mark didn't know what Dad did for a living, but he knew Dad's alternating sequence of color-coordinated suits. Shoes that matched the belts. Jackets that matched the pants. He knew that Dad worked for a big company. Software something or other. Terms like *analyst* and *coding* and *knowledge acquisition* slipped sometimes into Dad's anecdotes. Mark thought that Dad must buy and sell something intangible, immaterial. The exchange of concepts for commerce. Suits. Desks. Cubicles and offices in a downtown building.

Mark hung the wine glasses beneath the spice cupboard. "We learn about the history of the country. Mostly politics."

He heard the impact of glass meeting tile, a noisy collision.

"Jesus," Dad said. "Red alert." He cupped his hands around his mouth and made a shrill siren sound. "Seriously, Mark, watch your step. This is the problem with this tile floor, you know? Something so much as touches it today and we're still finding the pieces on Christmas eve."

Mark stepped back as Dad crouched down to collect the biggest pieces of debris. Dad brushed past him and muttered something about finding that goddamn broom.

"Do you need help?" Mark asked.

"I've got it under control," Dad said. Moments later he rushed back into the kitchen, wielding a blue plastic broom above his head and cocking a farcical grin. He swept the glass dust into a pile. "I hope they teach you something about the future in that class. And I'll tell you something else: you should start watching the news too. Start caring about this big blue world. Things are, well…things are not going so well. Do you ever watch the news?"

Mark answered this question at least three times a week, and his answer was always the same. "Not really."

"You should," Dad said. "You'd probably be surprised at some of the stuff going on in this country. In this *world.*"

Mark nodded like he understood.

Dad dumped the dustpan into the garbage pail beneath the sink and surveyed the area. "I'm going to vacuum," he said. "Just to be safe."

Chapter 5

MOM PREPARED A HEALTHY MEAL DESPITE Dad's pleas: white bean salad, brown rice, and pan-grilled salmon.

"I know it's good for me and all that," Dad said, raising his eyebrows. "It's just too bad it isn't as delicious as a carton full of Wong's fried rice."

Mom didn't smile. "If you want to have Wong's every night, you can pay for it."

"I'm kidding, dear." Dad laughed tersely and then looked down to focus on his plate. His perfectly mowed lawn still drifted visibly through his thoughts.

Mom kept glancing at Mark. Her silent expression said *I know something's up*, but Mark tried to avoid the looks. Kept his eyes on his food instead.

"How are Scott and Adam?" Mom asked.

"They're good," Mark said.

"Which one's Scott again?" Dad asked.

Nobody answered him. A squirrel chittered in the backyard. Dad shovelled beans into his mouth.

"Are you boys doing anything tonight?" Mom asked.

"No, Scott has to do housework," Mark said.

"Who's Scott?" Dad tried again.

Mom ignored him and kept her focus on Mark. "That's too bad. Will you be seeing them tomorrow?"

"Have I met Scott?" Dad asked.

"We might do something tomorrow," Mark said to Mom. "We'll see."

"Which one's Scott?" Dad nearly yelled.

Mark feigned attention as the conversation switched gears: There was a young couple who'd just moved in down the street, Mom reported, and she thought it might be a nice idea to have them over for dinner. Dad said yes, that would be good, and he tried to remember whether their liquor cabinet was appropriately stocked.

After dinner, Dad promptly collected the plates and left the room. While the sink was running, he turned on the miniature kitchen TV and tuned in to a hockey game, commentating under his breath. "Come on, try passing. Yes. That's it. Oh, so close…"

Mom fixed an expectant look on Mark. He pretended not to notice until she finally said something. "So how have you been, Mark?"

Mark no longer had a plate to gaze into, and so he did what he had to do. He made eye contact with Mom. "I've been good."

Just don't ask me how math is going and don't offer me a tutor and please, please don't ask if I need to start seeing a therapist again.

"Is school going well?" Mom asked. "Dad said you two were talking about your history class earlier."

"Yeah, we were talking about social studies," Mark said.

"Oh, he mentioned something about your history class," Mom said, and her tone of voice suggested that something else was on her mind altogether.

Mark suspected that he might get out of this conversation alive. "It's called social studies," he said.

"Mm. How are your other classes?"

"They're good, Mom."

Mom looked down now. She rotated her wedding band; flicks of light whispered off the wall. It was a habit she'd had for as long as Mark could remember. Whenever a conversation lulled, whenever things became uncomfortable or quiet, Mom spun the ring. Slowly. Almost methodically.

Looking at Mom, Mark suddenly remembered an incident from his early childhood when, late one evening in early November, he'd snuck downstairs to excavate his stash of Halloween candy. His parents always kept it hidden in the kitchen pantry, so that he couldn't binge-eat himself to sickness.

On his way to the kitchen, he'd seen a group of people standing outside. The group was close to the front lawn of his house, and so he stopped at the living room window, night-shaky and skin tingling. These people were older than Mom and Dad. Rough-looking men and women. Thick people, denim and leather, clouds of coughed steam, dense smoke, and vicious language. They were making a lot of noise. One of the women was flipping her waist-length hair back and forth, like a manic flag. She saw Mark staring and rushed at the window.

Tears sprung to Mark's eyes. Fear tears. He jumped back, but he couldn't completely peel away from her gaze. That coyote stare. Hungry eyes. She thumped on the window and yelled words that Mark was told to never say. Words like *fuck* and *shit* and *bitch*, words like *Watch me break through this fuckin' window and make you eat your own little raisin cock you fuckin' cunt brat.*

Mark ran upstairs to tell Mom and Dad. By the time they made their way to the living room, though, the crowd had disappeared. Later, when the police were asking Mom for a description she couldn't give, a description she simply did not have, she had stared down at her hands and fiddled with her wedding ring, cool and distant but visibly aware.

She wore the same look now as she'd worn then.

"Is anything wrong?" she asked finally.

Here we go. "What do you mean?" Mark said.

"You're my kid," Mom said. "I know you."

"I know."

"Okay, so what?"

Don't let on that anything's different. She's always got something going on in her own life. If you play it cool long enough, she'll back off and say that she needs a vacation.

"What?" Mark said.

"What's going on?"

"What do you mean?"

"You're acting, you know, strange."

Which is what you've said every time I go without smiling for longer than ten minutes, ever since I stopped seeing Dr. Broadrick. "Strange? How?"

"I don't know," Mom said. "You've been acting strange since I got home."

"How?"

"You just seem off."

"Off."

"You're quiet."

"I'm usually quiet," Mark said honestly.

"I know, but—"

"I'm not off."

Mom maintained her stare, extended it, rupturing Mark's guise.

He shifted in his chair, glanced back at her. Shrugged. "I don't know," he said.

Mom's stare, a probing, warding the Shack into his subconscious.

"Have you met any special girls?" she asked.

Dr. Broadrick always encouraged me to "be open to the possibilities of 'new friends'."

Madeline flitted through Mark's mind, and her smile, a simple memory, vague and warm, calmed him. "No," he said. "No girls."

"You should ask somebody out sometime," Mom said. "I'm sure there are lots of girls who would kill to go out on a date with you. Or boys, you know, if that's your thing. Your father and I don't care." She began spinning her wedding band again, then stopped to give Mark a final, imploring look. "You would tell me if something was up, right?"

"Of course," Mark said.

"You promise?"

"Of course."

"Say you promise."

"I promise. Of course I promise."

What else do I have to promise? That I won't hurt myself? That I won't hurt anyone else? It wouldn't be the first time.

To Mark's surprise, though, there were no more questions for now. Mom crossed the room and left, her face dissatisfied. Mark cleared the serving dishes from the table. As he did, he searched his mind for the root of Mom's suspicion. He was sure he'd washed all the blood from his face; Dad would've been the first to notice if it was still there. Yes, Dad would've showed him what a real tough guy looked like. Would've maybe rattled his buzz-sawed head off his skinny neck.

Sometimes Mom just knew.

Later, in the hallway between his parents' room and his own, Mark kissed Mom good night and nodded good night to Dad. He watched their bedroom door as it closed and he stood silently, waiting to see their lights go out. Once their room went dark, he waited an additional forty-five minutes, just to be safe. It was a specific, calculated amount of time. He checked his digital alarm clock every few minutes, shaking with anticipation.

He would see it again soon.

His bed was an uncomfortable tangle, too-short sheets, the mattress too firm one minute and too lumpy the next. He flipped and stirred. He stopped to count breaths. He tried to meditate in the waiting period.

The red digits on his clock taunted him. Dared him.

Once the designated amount of time had passed, he padded out of his room, shaking more violently now.

He stepped outside and was jolted by the coldness. The air didn't come in a blast, but in a wash, like waves of something cleansing, something soothing; it wrapped around his skinny body, slipped under his shirt and gusted over his stomach.

He ran out of the cul-de-sac, his sneakers recklessly slapping the pavement. His shadow was a giant under the streetlights, black pole legs skipping across the street. He was still shaking while he ran. He pushed his body, mind putting matter into a submission hold, and he ran faster. The shakes became tremors. Rattled his body as he sprinted down the sidewalk. He kept going. Tried to run the shakes away. He ran until dull pain came thudding back into his chest.

He thought Clinton must have knocked some bone fragments into his heart or something. His abdomen and chest flared. His run was reduced to a walk after some time, but he moved as quickly as he could manage, ignoring the intermittent stabs of pain.

Although he had only ever walked to the Shack from Adam's place, he knew, somehow, how to get there. He arrived within half an hour and, at a distance, he stared at the Shack for a while. He tried to allow his pain to subside, but it persisted in sharp ebbs and sharper flows.

The Shack was a colorless mound of non-specifics. It wasn't very big, but it wasn't very small either. It looked unfathomably welcoming, blank and untouched in the absence of light. Taken all at once, it was untraditionally beautiful, the way a dead bird is beautiful. He needed to look at it, even though he knew somehow that it should be left to itself. Left to fade into the ground.

He approached slowly, and a soft, comforting sensation brushed over him as he touched the door. Like embracing a grandfather he'd heard stories about, but who he'd never had the chance to meet. The walls of his throat clung together until he could barely breathe. He shivered. He ran his fingers along the seams of the door. Caressed flakes of peeling bark. He found the right spot, slipped his fingers inside, and pulled. Something crunched and gave way.

The door opened.

All his discomfort faded as he stepped inside. Not in an instant, no, but in smoothly subtle movements. His pain, now dim, disappeared with similar subtlety. He inhaled. Smelled the musty air. He walked further inside, trembling. He rested his back against a wall and slid to a sitting position, then set his hands on the floor, palms down. The dust and grit rubbed into his skin, and it excited him.

This place was different when he was alone. With Scott and Adam, the Shack always fell to the wayside; his friends were preoccupied with tobacco and puberty. Mark liked to smoke, and he liked to shoot the shit with his friends, but they could do those things anywhere. The Shack wasn't just a hangout spot; it wasn't just some hotbox haven for horny banter and cigarette smoke.

No, it was something else.

Mark wanted to climb the stairs, but he knew, somehow, that it would be better to let that wait. He didn't want to see it all at once. He sat for a long time before rising back to his feet. He walked into the nearest room; inside, there was a small window emblazoned with ragged old shutters. Otherwise it was empty.

Physically empty.

He wondered, vaguely, how he had never noticed the window before.

After a few dazed and silent hours had passed, he decided it was time to head home. It wasn't light out yet, but it was less dark than it'd been when he'd left.

The walk home was dizzying. His mind was clear, the air warmer. There was no longer even a whisper of pain in his body.

Arriving home, he opened the door with caution and crept back to his room. He slipped into bed.

Masturbated.

Chapter 6

MARK WALKED TO ADAM'S PLACE EARLY the next day. He knocked on the door and heard Adam's dad say, "Come in."

He stepped in with hesitation. It was strange entering someone's home when the door wasn't opened for him; the movement from everyone's outside to one family's inside seemed almost like an act of violence, like a violation. The doorway was a barrier, one that could only be lifted by a welcoming gesture. Although Mark had been friends with Adam since kindergarten, the feeling of discomfort stayed.

As he stepped inside, he saw Adam's dad sitting upright on the sofa. It had been so long since Adam's father had been employed, but he looked to Mark like the vice president of some prestigious firm. His shapely jaw was expertly shaved, his hair groomed and styled; his striking blue eyes reflected whatever old movie was playing on the TV. He ran his fingers through his slicked 'do and sighed, almost melancholy sounding, then took a sip from the glass of red wine that he cupped daintily in his hand.

He coughed into his fist. "How are you feeling today, Mark?"

"I'm good," Mark said. "You?"

"Very well." Adam's dad smiled. "But this film isn't impressing me." He laughed.

Mark looked at the TV. Widescreen. High definition. A washed-up actor screaming his way into the jaws of an animated monster. As the actor's belly was chewed into a pulp of hot sauce and spray-painted garden hose, Mark found himself wondering where else he'd seen that famous, screaming face. The prosthetics were outlined in pristine visual quality. Expensive stereo speakers rattled with the crunch of bones under teeth. So clear it was like you were there.

"Excellent speakers, though. I just got these recently," Adam's dad said. "You hear that? I mean, Lord Almighty, that's what a film is supposed to sound like."

Screaming. Synthesized music. Growly basilisk roars. The overbearing crackle of fangs crushing ribs.

"Do you hear that?" Adam's dad asked, nearly whispering.

"Yeah," Mark said. "That's great."

"Have you seen this actor before? He was quite strong in this one film…spy picture from uh…oh goodness, it'll come to me. You know the one. The one with uh, the woman with the exquisite ass. Oh goodness, what was it called…"

"I can't remember."

"Anyway, this film's basically a poor man's version of *Pet Sematary*, isn't it? There really hasn't been a good horror picture since *Pet Sematary*. Even the sequel was trash."

"I like some of the new ones," Mark said vaguely.

"Ah, the things you kids are watching have got *nothing* on the classics. What happened to the days of Carpenter? Argento? *Prince of Darkness*, *Suspiria*, *Elm Street*, you know, Wes Craven, Romero, all those wonderfully crazy guys…"

Mark paused, then said, "I saw a good new movie called *Cabin Fever*."

"I've never seen that one," Adam's dad said. "What is it, one of those teens in the woods slashers? There are enough *Friday the 13th* sequels to last two lifetimes. They should just let it be."

"Jason Voorhees is scary," Mark said.

"My goodness, Mark, if you think *Friday the 13th* is scary, wait until you see that one about the man who fucks corpses. *Beyond the Darkness*? Yes, that's the one."

"Never heard of it," Mark said.

Adam's dad laughed. Mark didn't understand why.

"I think Adam's downstairs," Adam's dad said.

Mark started to walk downstairs when Adam's dad stage-whispered to him, "Hey, Mark, would you like a glass of Malbec?"

Mark wasn't sure if it was a joke or not. Adam's dad just stared with his piercing, half-drunk eyes. His slanted smile made him looked roguishly handsome, almost boyish.

"Uh, sure," Mark said, and stepped forward.

Adam's dad stifled his laughter. "Get down there, you little delinquent."

Mark shrugged, turned, and walked down to Adam's room.

Adam was sitting in his desk chair, thumbing a controller, semi-conscious gaze fixed on his own TV screen, which was significantly smaller than his dad's.

"What's up?" Adam said without turning.

"Nothing much," Mark said.

Mark considered mentioning his conversation with Adam's dad, but decided against it; whenever Mark said anything about Adam's dad, Adam developed a temporary but decidedly unsettling stutter.

Mark sat on the bed and looked around the room. Adam's walls were collaged with pictures of women. Models. Actresses. Singers. Adam didn't know most of the women's names; he put them on his walls so he could stare at their bodies. Each photograph exploited its own form of anatomically specific arousal. Blondes. Brunettes. White women. Black women. Mark always took a passive interest in the photographs, but he'd never considered the process of application until now. Adam must've put a lot of time into finding these pictures; he must've spent hours flipping through pages, in search of images to appeal to his fantasies of the moment. Mark imagined Adam rooting through his dad's magazines: men's rags like *Sports Illustrated*, *Maxim,* and, of course, *Playboy* and *Hustler.* He imagined Adam's feverish eyes scanning the pages, seeking an advertisement or photo spread with enough flesh to satisfy his aims.

Sometimes Adam's dad would come into the room and make comments about the pictures; he seemed oblivious of their origin. He would point out specific women, look at Mark with arched eyebrows, and say something like, "It wouldn't be so bad to get a mouthful of that, now would it?"

Mark laughed at the comments. Adam ignored them; he played his video games and listened to his music, both at a high volume, competing with the eternally blasting television upstairs. He never replied.

Adam dropped the video game controller and turned to Mark. "So what do you want to do?"

"I don't know," Mark said. "Whatever the fuck we want, right?"

Adam looked around his room, silent for a moment. "I should call Scott too."

"Nah, don't bother," Mark said.

"Why not?"

Because he's a baby killjoy who won't let me go where I want to go.

Mark hesitated. "I don't want to put up with him right now."

"Jesus, are you still upset?" Adam asked.

"No, I just don't want to put up with him right now."

"What is it with you?"

"With me?"

Why is everyone always asking me the same fucking question?

"Yeah, you know, with you," Adam said clumsily. "Fuck it, Mark. Let's go tonight, all right?"

"Go," Mark said. "Tonight."

"Yeah. You know. To the fucking shack."

Mark was taken aback by the suggestion. *Too late, Adam. It's not ours anymore. That's my spot now.*

"No," he said.

Adam cawed a laugh of disbelief. "Are you kidding me right now? That's what you're doing, you're just fucking with me, right? Aren't you?"

"Just drop it, all right?"

And, quite unexpectedly, Adam did exactly what he was told, and he dropped it. He went back to his video game and Mark plugged in another controller.

"Start another game," Mark said. "Let me play against you."

After a few hours had passed, the sounds started upstairs: disagreements about an unpaid bill. *Get off your ass and do something for once, for Christ's sake*, the TV remote clacking against the table, *I look for work every day and the world gives me nothing, don't even think of coming home to give me your women's lib nonsense, I've got enough to deal with.* Silence for a while, then the voices returning. Muffled this time, entombed in another room. A cupboard cracking shut. The television, loud as ever, blaring monstrous growls and B-list screams. Adam's dad was yelling now, this time about the dishes or *why're you always on my case* or *where's the goddamn bill, give it to me and I will pay the goddamn thing.*

Adam ignored the sounds. Or, at least, he looked like he was ignoring them. Mark couldn't do the same; hairs raised on the back of his neck as the shouting intensified. It was like hearing the buried cadaver of his own parents' marriage coming to life. His mind fizzled with hideous flashback fragments: a barbecue night altercation, when Adam's dad had squeezed his wife's face between his thumb and forefinger, leaving bloody trails of ground beef all over her shaking features. When she'd opened her mouth to say *stop*, he'd pushed a wad of the red meat onto her tongue and she'd spewed vomit all over the kitchen floor. Mark also remembered Adam's dad locking Adam in the garage in mid-February for an entire night and saying, *If you try to come* in *here or get* out *of there, I will have to crack your shins with this hammer*, and then smiling at Mark upon his helpless departure.

The shouts got louder. A kitchen chair scraped linoleum and thudded against something. Adam kept playing his game, eyes vacant, until Mark set his controller down to look at him.

"What are you doing, man?" Adam said. "You're going to lose."

"Sorry. I can't concentrate," Mark said.

"Fuckin' all right, then." Adam turned off the console. "So what do we do, then?"

Stomping feet. He was sick of this nonsense, and she was crying.

"Let's go to Scott's place," Mark said.

"I thought you just said you don't want to see him. Make up your mind, for Christ's sake."

"I've made up my mind and I want to go see Scott."

"We could just fucking call him and ask him to come here," Adam said.

"No, let's go over there. The weather is good, so we can walk."

Adam mock-punched Mark, half looking like he wanted to *really* punch Mark. "Okay, fine. Fuck it. Whatever."

They walked upstairs. Adam's dad was sitting on the couch again; he was onto the next glass of Malbec. Adam's mother was crying in a room unknown to Mark.

As they were putting on their shoes, Adam's dad lifted himself from the couch with a groan that indicated strained muscles.

He watched them preparing to leave. "Where are you boys off to?"

"Out," Adam said. "Going to Scott's place."

"Are you going to meet up with some girls?" his dad asked, ruffling Mark's hair with a damp hand.

Wordlessly, Adam stepped outside. Mark fumbled with his shoes.

"So, what's the story?" Adam's dad asked. "Are you seeing some little cuties or what?"

The crying was a horrible and persistent frequency in the background. It wasn't unharnessed wailing; it was the kind of raspy sobbing that leaves your stomach nauseous and your head feeling light. Physical, taxing, from the guts.

Mark's heart thumped. He finally got his shoes on. "I guess we'll see."

Adam's dad clapped once. Mark forced a smile and started to turn toward the door.

"Oh, Mark, before you go, I have a question for you," Adam's dad said.

If you *are about to ask me if anything's wrong, I think I might just lose it right here right now.*

Mark nodded, avoiding the sticky, intoxicated stare. He stared at the floor.

"Would you like some of this?" Adam's dad asked, holding the wine toward him, wavering, sweating.

What was the proper reply? *Just don't say anything at all.* "No, I'm okay." Mark's voice was weak, pathetic, low.

Adam's dad sputtered a wet laugh. "Okay, have fun. Be safe. Don't be out too late, wear a condom, blah blah blah, all that sort of stuff."

"See you later," Mark said.

He stepped outside, and as he shut the door, he could have sworn he saw something a lot like sadness on Adam's face. Mark thought again about the garage, so cold that Adam could've died.

Adam's expression vanished with the kind of swift and conscious determinacy that only a kid raised in some approximation of hell could manage. He did it so fast, with such finesse, that Mark thought maybe he'd just imagined the sadness.

Chapter 7

THEY TOOK THE BUS TO SCOTT'S place. Approaching the door, they heard the sound of a vacuum humming underneath classic rock radio. Mark rang the bell. The vacuum switched off and the volume of the music went down. Scott's dad swung the door open. He removed his square glasses and wiped them on the front of his shirt. He wore a superficial smile. An *I don't trust you* smile.

"Hi, is Scott home?" Mark asked.

"He sure is. Come on in." Scott's dad peered over Mark's shoulder to grace Adam with a big and genuine grin, a grin that said, *Aww shucks, kid, shame about your parents, I can be a Father Figure for you.*

"You too, Adam," Scott's dad said. "Don't be a stranger."

Mark and Adam stepped inside, and Scott's dad exited the room to get Scott. The house was museum clean. The rug was newly replaced; sunlight glowed off the living room coffee table's dark wood surface. A picture of high real estate value and familial joy.

Scott greeted Mark and Adam, a dust cloth dripping in his hands. "Hey, guys, what's up?"

"Nothing much," Mark said. "Just wondering if you want to hang out with us."

Scott turned to look at his dad, who had started vacuuming again. "You mind, Dad?"

"When are you going to finish your chores?" his dad asked.

"We won't be gone long," Scott said.

Scott's dad fixed Mark with a distrusting look, then shrugged at Scott. Scott looked at Mark with pleading eyes and Mark stared blankly back.

"Let's go," Mark said.

Scott relented and they went outside.

"What's going on?" Scott hissed. "I told you I have chores to do."

"Shut the fuck up and come on. Let's do something," Adam said.

Scott pressed his lips together, and as they walked out of the cul-de-sac, he mumbled something about putting Mark in his place.

Scott and Adam were prepared to waste a day in the sun.

Mark, convincing in motion and speech, was someplace else.

***

Clinton was still pissed off on Monday morning.

Watching him lumber across the field, Mark wished Adam and Scott were there. Maybe they'd be willing to back him up this time—he was pretty damn sure he hadn't started anything.

Clinton stopped in front of him, hugging distance. "Say you're sorry."

"What?" Mark said.

"Say you're fucking sorry."

"You're fucking sorry."

A beefy forearm caught Mark in the ribs; he'd once heard this particular action described as the *dry gulch*. Whatever it was called, it hurt. He stumbled back and crumpled into himself, the blow lingering in his ribcage, clenching his lungs and slowing his breath. He tried, again, to remember what joke he'd first made to set Clinton off, and he failed, again, to recall. He wheezed and coughed and he couldn't focus through the pain. The kid could definitely land a hit.

But Mark wouldn't back down. That would make him this war's loser.

"Say it," Clinton said.

Mark landed what he hoped was a menacing glare. "Fuck you."

Clinton's face contorted into a cartoon scowl, his eyebrows a deep V, his mouth an upturned rainbow. He looked hesitant for an instant, but quickly rearranged his expression and kicked. His Converse, size Infinity, clipped Mark in the balls; the pain jolted upward to settle in Mark's guts, his testicles numb with instant pain. As he hit grass, he caught a glimpse of Madeline.

She was standing far away. Practically on the other end of the field, but he knew it was her. For a moment he thought she smiled. That smile. The smile that was just for him. Mark considered that maybe she could see him, even from this distance. He imagined how ridiculous he looked, balled up on the grass, nursing his crotch, his face a portrait of defeat.

Humiliation was the antidote to pain. He managed to ignore his aching nuts and his soon-to-be-bruised ribcage. He jumped to his feet and lunged.

His head moulded into Clinton's damp, warm stomach.

Mark dove fast enough and hard enough that Clinton lost his footing and dropped. He gave an oxygen-stopping *whoof* as he connected with the ground. Mark's groin pulsed, nausea thrusting through his insides. He focused on the thought that maybe Madeline was watching, and he straddled Clinton's broad abdomen.

He took a clumsy swing and his knuckles connected with the left side of Clinton's head. Clinton yelped. Mark hooked a left and cracked Clinton on the other temple. His knuckles were singing crazy songs; the skin was scuffed already, beads of blood rising through.

Clinton clapped meaty hands to his ears and screamed. "Are ya crazy? I'm gonna go deaf."

Mark responded with an awkward but solid jab, straight down on Clinton's face. Clinton's broad lips spread apart from the blow. A canine split Mark's middle finger open. Saliva frothed on his bleeding fist.

Mark was in character now: the man on top.

Clinton was too large to be held down; he emitted a teary, high-pitched yowl that made Mark's ears scream in sync. Clinton wobbled like a giant earthworm. He was strong enough and wet enough to make Mark slip from his belly and thump to the ground.

Clinton collected himself with a series of damp wheezes and breathless obscenities. He lunged at Mark, gigantic hands spread like catcher's mitts.

One palm clapped around Mark's esophagus and clutched. Air sprung from Mark's mouth with the sound of a backward gulp. He clawed at Clinton's wrists. Instinctive, frantic.

Mark's panic intensified as Clinton's grip tightened, tightened, tightened. Mark sunk his fingernails into the moist meat of Clinton's forearm, burrowed like a clam digger sifting through sand. Clinton howled and eased his grip. Blood dribbled under Mark's fingernails. Clinton let his guard down for an instant to clutch his bleeding forearm, and Mark took advantage.

He arced his fist and clubbed Clinton on the forehead. Clinton dropped like a pile of linen, facedown. Mark pinned him, now seething, muttering, his eyesight blotted from oxygen loss. He reached around to grab Clinton's face. His index finger slid into Clinton's mouth and Clinton chomped. Mark's skin broke, his cartilage straining from the pressure. He fought through the pain, mounting crimson and vivid. He formed forceps with his pointer finger and thumb, closing them around Clinton's molar. He pulled. He yanked and strained, thinking only of the urgent need to release his finger.

There was a horrible, sucking resistance as his hand, drenched in spit and blood, pulled free.

He dropped Clinton's tooth on the grass as he sprang back. He looked down at the tooth and, in sickening vividness, he saw pink nerve tissue clinging to the end of it.

"Holy fuck," he said.

He felt as if he might faint or vomit or both when, a moment later, hands gripped his armpits from behind. They were grownup hands.

"Leave him alone," a woman's voice cried. "What is wrong with you?"

Panicked, shrill: he recognized the voice right away as Ms. Corr's. He scanned the field for Madeline as he was hoisted away from Clinton's massive, writhing body. He couldn't see her anymore.

While still clutching Mark's arm with lacquered fingernails, Ms. Corr pulled a moaning Clinton to his feet; blood had painted his chin red.

"Look at all this blood," Ms. Corr moaned.

Clinton wept and said, "Thank God, just keep him off me."

Mark had the feeling that this was real trouble. He'd been in real trouble many times, yes, and this is what it felt like: a sinking affect. There was always the post-fight shaking, a mixture of adrenaline, shame, and fear, his body rattling with the dregs of aggression and the nefarious realization that the excitement, if it could be called that, was over.

Now it was time for the phone call to his parents, and Mark knew that Mom and Dad were long since fed up with his fighting. In fact, mere months after he'd stopped *needing time with Dr. Broadrick*, he'd heard their muffled bedroom conversations, phrases like, *I think he's starting to turn himself around, he's really been trying lately.* He attempted to squash his fear, looking coldly ahead as the white-faced teacher pulled him toward the school.

She dropped the two boys on a bench outside the principal's office. She stooped in front of them. Within such close proximity, Mark noticed that one of her eyelids was painted darker than the other.

"Not a word," she said, darting her eyes from Mark to Clinton. "My goodness, all the blood..."

She heel-clicked away.

When she was safely out of earshot, Clinton turned to glare at Mark and pressed a palm to his mouth, scarlet, heaving with ragged gasps. "All ya had ta do was apologize, ya idiot."

Mark looked down at his hands; they were still quivering, blood-streaked.

Principal Weatherill emerged from her office. She was a stout, bulky woman with gray hair, a gray dress, and a grayer demeanour. She looked like she'd been interrupted in the middle of a great TV mystery. Mark wondered what it was that the principal did in her office; how many phone calls did she and *could* she make and take on any given day? How many documents could she type?

"Come into my office, Mark," Mrs. Weatherill said. "Clinton, wait there."

Mark followed her.

He remembered his first visit to the office, when he'd tipped a garbage can in the hall for the sake of making a loud noise. When he'd first sat down, Mrs. Weatherill had given him the same look she was giving him now. She reclined in her office chair, wheeling backward slightly, gray eyes that never seemed to blink in the presence of others. The pre-conversation waiting period, in which Mark was expected to break down into tearful apologies. Instead, he stared back blankly, waiting for the diagnosis.

"How are things at home, Mark?" Mrs. Weatherill asked. "Anything change since we last spoke? Parents okay?"

"Fine," Mark said.

Weatherill's eyelids fluttered half-shut and, for a moment, she looked like her eyeballs had rolled back into her head. She rocked soundlessly.

The principal's office must've been the most soundproof room in the school. Mark's eyes always drifted to the same spot, a window behind Weatherill's head; one time, he'd seen two students smashing the shit out of someone's car with golf clubs and lead pipes, a drug deal gone wrong, and even then he couldn't hear a thing. This room was quiet enough to hear the quiet, and the quiet sounded like static, broken only by the ticking and tocking of a grandfather clock, a piece of bizarre decor stationed to the left of the window.

"Ms. Corr wants you expelled," Weatherill said flatly.

Mark said nothing.

"What do you think of that?" she asked. "Think you should be expelled? We reach that point yet?"

Mark picked at the skin around his fingernail. Caught himself in the absentminded act and looked back up at Weatherill. "I don't think I should be expelled."

Weatherill lifted a coffee mug, unsteaming, from her desk. She slurped a mouthful with a mild grimace and exhaled. She set the mug down and reached for the phone with her other hand.

"Doesn't think he should be expelled," she said, staring with a strange fixation at her filing cabinet. "The question of expulsion. Something we'll have to discuss with your parents."

By now, she had memorized Mark's home number. Mark's mind wandered to the Shack as she dialed. It wouldn't be so bad to get expelled. He wouldn't have to put up with his bullshit classes every day, wouldn't have to deal with this bullshit routine all the time.

Mark could hear his mother's voice on the other end of the line, dim but distinct.

Weatherill gazed deskward, furrowed her gray brow. "Hello, it's Mrs. Weatherill calling." A pause. "Yes, I'm afraid so." A longer pause. Her lips thinned gravely. "It's come to the question of expulsion. That's right, the question. Yes. Of expulsion. If you'd just come down here. Yes. Okay, bye."

There was yet another pause, she gave an emotionless "thank you," and she placed the phone on the receiver. "She should be here in a while. Go tell Clinton."

Mark waited for her to continue for nearly half a minute before asking, "Tell him what?"

"Like to have a word with him," Weatherill spoke somehow through sealed lips. "You can wait outside."

Mark realized he was picking at his skin again. He gave Weatherill a blank look.

The Shack was somewhere above, in, or below his mind, smothering any semblance of fear. This whole clusterfuck would be resolved at some point, and when it was, the Shack would still be there.

He walked out of the office and looked at Clinton, a dripping lump on the bench. Clinton sniffled and wiped sweaty tears from his cheeks. He looked up at Mark and scowled. Exhaled hissing breath through clenched teeth, blood drying on his broad chin. Guard dog face.

"My dad died, asshole," he said.

"Weatherill is waiting for you," Mark said.

"My dad died."

"I already apologized."

"Ya can't just say sorry once," Clinton said. "It doesn't just go away."

"What do you want, then?" Mark said.

Clinton drooped, deflated. "Ya… Jesus, ya don't understand."

Mark looked at Clinton's doughy, agonized face, felt nothing, and shrugged. Clinton hoisted himself to his feet, leaving a stamp where he'd sat. He thudded against Mark, nearly knocking him off his feet, and made his way to the office. Mark sat down, careful to avoid the wet spot.

He'd only been sitting for a moment when Madeline walked down the hall, heading toward him. She checked the hallway both ways for teachers or supervisors. When she confirmed the coast was clear, she stopped in front of him.

She was wearing a striped sweater, pink and red. Black leggings. Studded choker. Hair tied back. Eyes fixed, but not invasive: coolly, almost blandly, knowing.

"So what'd you do this time?" she asked, not smiling. Not even close to smiling.

"What do you mean by that?" he replied.

She made a *pfft* sound. "You're always getting in trouble. Everybody knows that."

Mark shrugged and fidgeted. "I just do stupid things. I don't know why."

"Have you ever considered that maybe it's because you're stupid?" Madeline said.

He fidgeted more, realized he was slouching, and straightened up. Slouched again. "Yeah, maybe I am."

She smiled, finally. "I'm just fucking with you. Calm down."

Her eyes drifted to his bleeding hands and her smile blinked out and Mark immediately missed it.

"Wow, you guys weren't just joking around, huh?" she said.

"No," Mark said. "He wants to kill me."

"Fighting's not cool, man."

She didn't sound impressed or amused; on the contrary, Mark thought her tone sounded pretty close to disgusted.

"Yeah, well, what choice do I have when a guy who's forty times my size wants my head?" he asked. He was still fidgeting, his motions spastic and clumsy. Trying to wipe half-dried blood from his knuckles and getting it smeared all over his palms instead.

"Well," Madeline said, "I think you should stop fighting, because you seem like you could be an all right person, and not a stupid person."

"What makes you say that?" Mark asked.

"I don't know. You always smile at me. Nobody smiles at me."

Mark looked her in the eyes. Smiling eyes, unsmiling mouth.

"I should go to class," Madeline said. "It looked like the warden was giving you some visitation time, so I thought I would take advantage, because what the hell."

"Thanks," Mark said, and meant it.

She walked away.

She'd actually spoken to him. Before he could allow the pleasant shock to register, Mom arrived, sunglasses pierced through her fanned-out hair, her lips pressed together.

A moment after she entered, Clinton stamped out of the office; he'd gone from wet to moist. He wiped his wrist across his eyes, looked at Mom, then at Mark. He stomped away and said, "This is all bullshit."

Weatherill emerged from the office and directed a gray stare at the space between Mark and Mom. "Both of you can come into my office," she said. She disappeared into the room.

Mark rose from the bench and Mom advanced toward him. "You're not in the sandbox anymore, last time I checked," she said. "It's probably time to grow up now, don't you think?"

"I know. I'm sorry," Mark said.

"You *could* say you're sorry. Or you could actually, you know, *grow up.*"

Mom strode into Weatherill's office and Mark trailed close behind. They sat beside each other, across from Weatherill.

"Okay, so. You've been here before. We all know this," Weatherill said.

Mom rubbed a palm against her forehead. "We all know this, yes."

Weatherill nodded and stared at Mark. A gray silence descended on the room.

Mom patted Mark on the kneecap. "We all know this, don't we?"

"I know," Mark confirmed.

"Violence is a pattern," Weatherill said. She paused, allowing the vague gravity of her sentiment to set in. "Mark has been here many times. Uncountable. I could count if I consulted the records. The documents. We now have the question of expulsion. I don't want to see that happen, expulsion. But violence…these things, these issues, get to the point where—"

"The point where what?" Mom said.

"The point where questions are raised."

Mom narrowed her eyebrows and leaned in closer to Weatherill. Mark thought she might come to his defense, might chase Weatherill's distant, ominous suggestions a little further.

Instead, Mom only said, "We don't need to ask those kinds of questions. Mark's done with this nonsense." She turned to face Mark. "Right?"

Mark looked down at his hands; his dry blood looked like magma. "Right."

"Right," Mom said once more.

Weatherill took another gulp of her coffee, and Mark wondered how cold it must be at this point. "I've heard this. Mark, I've heard these things. From you. From others. How do I decide not to ask these questions? Why not expulsion? Why another chance?"

Mark forced himself to look at her. Her eyes were as emotionless as her filing cabinet.

"I mean it," he said. "That's really all I can say."

Weatherill raised the coffee cup, noticed it was now empty and set it back down. She tried to make the gesture look natural, but she failed. She slouched in her chair until it reclined almost horizontally, then brought herself back up. "Maybe we should bring in Clinton. His mother, too. The five of us sitting down. Why not raise the question of violence? 'Why violence?' Stop the cycle… What do you think?"

The queries were for no one in particular, an unscripted script fulfilled.

"This is my son," Mom repeated, and Mark heard an edge he'd never heard before. "There will be no more problems. My son is not a violent person." Her voice lilted a little as she finished her last sentence, and Mark quietly wondered if she'd ever really believed that.

"To be sure," Weatherill said, gazing now into the blackish crust at the bottom of her cup. "Mark. You will receive an informal suspension. One week."

Mark looked at Mom, who raised her hands and pointed to Weatherill. "Talk to her, kiddo. Don't look at me."

"What's an informal suspension?" Mark asked.

"A compromise. It's not expulsion. You're to stay home. One week," Weatherill replied. "I'll talk to your teachers. They will talk to me, and we will determine assignments. Homework that will last you the duration of that week. I will also ask you to write a report for me. I *am* asking you…telling you. This report will detail the negative effects of violence. Two thousand words. You need to think about this. That violence goes in circles. It goes up, then down, and then back around. A loop-de-loop."

Mark nodded, semi-hypnotized by his own hands again.

"Okay," Weatherill said. "Fighting is never the answer."

"Okay," Mom said. "Is that it, then?"

"That's it. We should say, though—*I* should say that Mark no longer has the liberty of a question. It is now a fact. We're looking at facts. If this happens again, it's expulsion. This school's policy indicates zero tolerance for violence," Weatherill said. "I want to be made clear. Am I?"

Mom looked at Mark. "Mark, is that clear?"

"Yes. That's clear," Mark said.

"Okay," Weatherill said, Judge Judy tone. "That's that. One week suspension."

Mom looked at Mark and gestured toward the door. She turned to Weatherill on her way out. "The last time. I promise you."

Mark walked through the hallway, Mom behind him.

As they moved, she uprooted the sunglasses from her hair and put them on. "I don't know what to do with you sometimes."

Mark heard exhaustion in her voice. Real, serious exhaustion. "Sorry, Mom," he said.

"Why apologize to me? Talk to that poor kid. What's his name? Clinton?"

They broke through the doors; Mom was practically jogging, and Mark now walked a few paces behind her.

"I apologized to him already," he said.

Mom turned to fix him with a no bullshit look. "I hope you did. I don't know when you had this sudden revelation that it's okay to hit people." She patted her jacket pockets and muttered, "Where the hell did I put my frigging keys?"

"I'm sorry," Mark said.

Mom found her keys and fumbled with the lock. "What does the word mean, *sorry*? What does the word actually mean to you?" She got into the car and snapped the door shut before Mark could attempt an answer.

He got in, buckled up his seatbelt. Mom drove to the edge of the parking lot and flicked her turn signal; it ticked between Mark's breaths.

"You told me that one of your classmates had a parent who passed away," Mom said.

"Yes," Mark said. He anticipated the next question, his gut clenching.

Mom paused to merge. Waved to the car that slowed so she could get into the lane. "That classmate was the boy you were fighting with today," she said.

"Yes," Mark said.

Mom inhaled deeply. Pressed her palm against her forehead again. "Oh man. Oh man, oh man, oh man."

Mark almost said he was sorry again, but said nothing instead. He turned his head and looked out the window; a middle-aged man was pushing a shopping cart full of garbage bags down the sidewalk.

"Mark, are you listening?" Mom asked.

"Yes," he said. "Of course."

"Okay, what's up? What's going on with you? You know that kid's been going through some really difficult stuff. Do you think you made it easier on him? His dad passed away. How do you think that would make you feel? If your father passed away and someone at school was giving you a hard time?"

Mark became aware of the engine's hum. He watched vehicles whizzing by. A pale, insistent pain brewed behind his eyes. "I know, Mom. I'm sorry."

Mom switched lanes, but this time she didn't wave to the car that made space for her.

"We used to talk," she said, letting the thought hang before continuing. "Do you ever ask yourself questions?"

"Questions?"

"Yes, questions," Mom said. "You should ask yourself some serious questions. You're not a bad person, Mark. Do you really want to act like one?"

Mark's forehead roasted with oncoming pain. "I know. I can change."

A traffic light turned red and Mom turned to look at Mark. She shook her head. Mark could see by her expression that she was finished—she'd crossed the threshold, and anything else she said was pure performance. Playing out a routine.

She rummaged through the glove compartment and unearthed a CD. The light turned green and she jolted in shock, dropping the disc on her lap. Eyes fixed ahead, she handed the CD to Mark. "Can you put this on, please?" she said. "I should be watching the road."

Mark slipped the disc into the player, and sentimental piano notes boomed promptly from the speakers. Mom twisted the volume knob to the right. Mark's head screamed in protest. A once-famous vocalist warbled about lost opportunities or divorce complications. Something about doors and wings in someone's heart. Mom's eyes went a little glassy.

Mark thought about a place with no name. A place that somehow existed someplace else.

Chapter 8

DAD WAS SPRAYING INSECT KILLER ON the lawn when they got home, meaty brow crumpled over his sunglasses. As the car pulled into the driveway, he lifted himself up and stood motionless on the grass, gripping the can of Raid in his soil-spattered hand.

Mark got out of the car first. He tried to read Dad's expression, but it was too difficult to see anything through those black sunglass lenses.

"I'm not exactly feeling thrilled with you," Dad said.

Mark imagined reflection Dad superimposed on real Dad, telling Mark he wasn't tough.

Mom got out of the car. "Go inside, Mark. We'll talk over dinner."

Mark walked into the house, went up to his room and sat on the edge of the bed. His head pulsed and throbbed, cadences of discomfort. He looked down at his hands, grimacing at the blackish crust on his knuckles. As he exited his room to clean himself up, he heard his parents talking in the kitchen, heard Mom saying his name. He crept closer to the banister and listened closely.

"...and whatever it is, I'm not sure what to do anymore..." Mom was saying.

"Maybe it's time to start yanking his privileges," Dad said. "This kid gets whatever he wants, whenever he wants, and that's no good. By his age, I was working full-time at Papa's gas station. And when I wasn't working, I was hitting the books. And when I wasn't reading, I was pumping weights."

"Well, I don't know about that..."

"I was pumping serious iron by his age, dear."

"...I mean I don't know that he gets whatever he wants."

"I do," Dad said. "If I had been starting this much trouble when I was his age, do you know what my papa would've done?"

"Come on," Mom said.

"No, seriously. He'd kick my fu— my frigging ass. He *did* kick my ass. A few times."

"I know, but that's not right," Mom said.

"I'm not saying it's right, but I *am* saying I learned my lesson. Remember how they used to use the strap in school? Little Billy thinks he's hot shit, yells out a curse word and *Whap!*, teacher whacks the attitude out of him."

"I don't think they *should* use the strap anymore," Mom said. "Whipping children isn't the answer, honey."

For Dad it very well might be… The costs of therapy are much, much higher than the cost of a belt. In fact, there are lots of belts already waiting; color-coordinated with the right suits, every one of them.

"Yeah, well, it sure as heck kept me in line," Dad said. "We're all just too delicate on our kids these days. I think we need to be harder on them, I'm telling you. Remind them how things *used* to be."

"I don't know. We will have to start taking his privileges away," Mom said.

Dad didn't sound satisfied. "Yeah, well, I'm not so sure that's going to be enough. He gets a little vacation, right? 'Informal suspension.' Give me a break! Maybe a bit of bruising would do him just fine."

"For God's sake," Mom said.

"I wouldn't do it, I'm just saying…"

"This isn't going to be a vacation," Mom promised. "He's going to be doing housework and homework."

"Yeah, well…"

"A lot of homework."

"Yeah, and we should take away some of his privileges, too. Like you were saying."

This is a recurring theme. The dreaded Privilege Removal—maybe something Dr. Broadrick suggested way back when. Emergency Parenting Technique #17.

"He's going to need a tighter leash," Mom agreed. "I hate to say it and I don't want to take that approach, but I just… I don't know what to do anymore."

Mark padded down the hall and into the bathroom. He took three extra strength Tylenols and washed them down with tap water. He took a hesitant glance in the mirror as he rubbed the scabs away.

"I'm one ugly little motherfucker," he muttered aloud. He turned off the tap, wiped his hands, and walked back into his room.

When dinner arrived, he sat wordlessly at the table. Stared at his plate of pork ribs, boiled potatoes, and steamed Brussels sprouts. His stomach churned with unease.

"So your father and I were just having a talk," Mom said.

"About what?" Mark asked; truth was, he didn't know what else to ask.

"About what happened today," Mom said.

"What's been happening for a while," Dad added.

"We're not going to tolerate it anymore," Mom said. "And we're not going to hold your hand, either. You're getting too old for all this. You're going to have to take more responsibility from now on. We can't keep letting this happen. And it's up to you to change it." She opened her mouth as if to add another thought, but she stopped herself. She placed her fork on the table and began rolling her ring between her fingers.

Dad frowned, chewing his food with terse, dramatic chomps. "No more Mr. Nice Guy."

Was it Mr. Nice Guy who reached out to grab my throat when I was seven years old, and looked like he was really about to strangle the life out of me? Was Mr. Nice Guy just unlucky that Mom got home before he could do what he wanted to do?

"We're going to take away some of your privileges," Dad said.

"Like what?" Mark asked.

Dad leaned forward in his chair. His jaw twitched; a vein probed the side of his neck. He gave Mark a silent challenge with his eyes. "What do you mean, *like what*? None of this should be news to you. You did this to yourself. Do you understand?"

"Yes, I understand," Mark said. "But what privileges do you mean?"

Dad looked at him with eyes like flint. "Little shitnosed wiseguy, huh?"

"Dear!" Mom said.

"I was only kidding, honey," Dad said. Then, after a pause, he pointed his fork at Mark; a saucy lump of meat dangled from its tines. "I don't want you around those kids all the time. You know, Adam and that other kid."

"Scott," Mark said.

Dad nodded once, as if the name had been just on the periphery of his memory. He rolled his massive shoulders and huffed. "Right, Scott... Is he the one?"

"Yes," Mark said. "Scott is the other guy."

"Okay then. Scott. You're not going to be running all willy-nilly with those two, causing who knows what kind of trouble while you're barely passing your classes. It's time to take away those privileges. Period."

Mark had the brief urge to stand up for his friends, but he couldn't force himself to muster the energy. He also thought it was in the very best of his own interest to shut up and listen. While Dad might look somewhat composed, Mark knew the truth. On some level, Dad really did want to stab something other than his dinner with that fork.

"This suspension isn't going to be a free ride, Mark," Mom said. "I want you doing homework all day, every day. In the evenings, you're going to be helping out around the house."

Mark's head was beginning to hurt again. He grimaced and shoveled a sprout into his mouth, not sure what to say. The silence dragged on too long, discomfort descending, and so he spoke. "When can I see my friends again?"

"When you've proved that we can trust you," Mom said.

"I'm sorry," Mark said.

A lump of pork bobbed in Dad's cheek, his vein receding, his face paling from scarlet to pink. "Sorry doesn't make it right, Mark. Actions, not words. That's what we want."

After dinner, Mark washed the dishes in silence. His headache was subsiding; in its place was an unrelenting anxiety. He kept replaying the conflict with Clinton. Kept seeing that tooth in the grass, the vivid pinkness of flesh in the sunlight. What would've happened if Ms. Corr hadn't stepped in? How much worse could it have been?

He shuddered, dropping the final dish into a sink full of hot rinse-water. As he turned to exit the room, he saw Dad step out from the darkness of the dining room. Mark looked at him, his pulse accelerating. Nowhere to run.

Dad glanced over his shoulder, checking to see if Mom was nearby. A familiar motion. He took two heavy steps toward Mark. Mark backed against the sink and the counter smacked his spine.

"Don't say a word," Dad warned, grabbing a handful of Mark's shirt, pulling him forward so hard that he nearly fell.

Suds leapt from Mark's hands and melted promptly on the tiles. Air escaped his lungs.

"Honey," Mom called from upstairs.

Dad maintained eye contact with Mark. "I'm not going to coddle you. Mommy coddles, Daddy gets the job done."

Mom called him again.

"Yeah, be right up," Dad hollered back. Then, with a smirk, he added, "I don't have the money for a long-distance call."

He turned to face Mark again, and his eyes said it all. Whatever he meant by *getting the job done*, Mark knew he didn't want to be on the receiving end. After what felt like an infinite minute, soundtracked only by the plopping of suds on the kitchen floor, Dad released him.

"Daddy gets the job done," Dad repeated in a weirdly sing-song tone. He smoothed the wrinkles he'd made on Mark's shirt, clapped his son on the cheek. Then, without pause, he pivoted on his heels and left as quickly as he'd entered.

Mark stood in the kitchen, collecting his breath. It had been a day of shaking. A day of violence and noise.

Chapter 9

MARK WOKE TO HIS MOTHER'S VOICE saying, "Okay kiddo, up you get. You've got lots to do today."

He raised his head to look at the alarm clock digits. 7 am. Fucking hell. He squinted toward his doorway, where Mom was standing.

She placed her hands on her hips. "Up. You. Get."

"I don't have to go anywhere today," he said.

"No, but that's not going to stop you from doing schoolwork, is it?"

Mark said nothing.

"Is it?" Mom repeated. "Did you already forget the talk we had last night?"

"My classes don't even start until nine."

"I don't care, Mark. You're getting up now." Mom walked away, leaving the door open.

Sunlight pressed through the front window and filled Mark's room. "God damn it," he grumbled.

He began to peel the sheets from his body, but he jerked his hand back in surprise. The linen was wet—not just damp, but completely soaked through. Still orienting himself in the harsh morning brightness, he noticed that his shirt and forehead were also moist. What little sleep he'd gotten had apparently caused him to sweat. A lot.

He shoved aside the sopping blankets and sat on the edge of the bed, cradling his face in his palms. He'd had a nightmare—his body tingled with the sensation…that feeling of being followed. Goosebumps rose on his bare flesh. Although he didn't want to remember, the nightmare came back.

He'd been walking through a field, retreating from something. It was a threat with no clear form, whose very *formlessness* carried with it a sense: persistence, relentless advance, potential harm. Mark's brisk dream-walk soon evolved into a run; he sprinted for an impossible amount of time, limbs pumping with violent panic. He was running faster than physical reality would ever allow when suddenly something gripped at his shoulder, something with fingers full of bone. He was yanked around, and what he saw simply could not be described. This part of the dream was unclear, and the only thing that Mark now remembered was that he'd felt nothing but pure, paralyzing dread. In the dream he'd been damned with the feeling—no, the knowledge—that he would never escape this thing. A heavy black cloud formed before him: putrid, excessively bleak. The cloud molded into something that he could not process, and the leering fog stared with impossible, eyeless menace. Mark could feel its judgment gazing outward, probing him for something.

Now, thinking about that fog in his uneasy morning haze, Mark suddenly remembered an event from his childhood. He'd been seven or eight, maybe, and he'd been home sick with the flu for nearly a week. One evening, Mom had left the house to buy him some canned chicken soup from the neighborhood grocery store. While she was gone, Mark flipped through the channels and arrived at a news story. A field journalist was jabbing his microphone at a white-haired man with a sagging face, a man who looked like he might be friends with Mark's grandfather.

"Did you consider how these parents felt?" the reporter asked. "How about the children?

How about the children you locked up? How about the children you kept in your basement?"

The old man hobbled away, his thin bangs fluttering in the breeze.

"How about the children?" the reporter persisted.

The old man wheeled around to face the reporter, who backed away several steps. The man's eyes were vacant, slate gray, cold but full of distant intelligence. Double zeroes. His voice was high-pitched and unassuming as he said, "I didn't do it, but even if I had, those children were street urchins and they probably deserved what they got. All those children will go to hell. Every one of them."

Through the screen, through miles of distance, through the gap of time between recording and airing, Mark had made eye contact with the killer/child molester/unknowable suspect. He had turned off the TV and stared at the black bubble of the dead screen, still seeing the trace of that man's face fading on the surface.

The fog in his nightmare had been something like that old man's stare, only much more immediate, much more powerful. Staring back at the threat, Dream Mark had screamed until his voice ceased to make noise. Until he'd screamed sound itself into extinction. He'd sobbed. He'd tried to pull himself away, but the grip was too strong. In his periphery, he'd seen the Shack, and he had sensed absence. Someone was gone. Someone close.

And someone was never coming back.

That was the last thing he remembered before Mom had burst in.

He shivered despite the room's warmth, rubbed his eyes and pried himself off the bed. He shuffled into the kitchen, where Mom was pouring milk into a cup of tea. She looked prepared to go out, her hair styled and her clothes neatly pressed.

"I'm leaving soon, Mark," she said, "but I don't want you doing anything except homework while I'm gone. Is that clear?"

"Yeah," Mark said. The nightmare was already fading from his memory, leaving the vaguest imprint behind. Right now, he was only interested in the fact that Mom would be gone. How long? That was the question.

Mom stirred her tea. "That means no TV, no leisure reading, nothing."

Mark sat at the kitchen table and surveyed the backyard, where it looked like Dad had forgotten to cut the grass in lieu of his focus on the front lawn.

Mom came up behind him and ruffled his hair. "Got it?"

"Yeah, I got it, Mom," Mark said. "Where are you going?"

Mom sat beside him and blew steam off her tea. "I'm visiting Joanne. I won't be gone very long."

"Okay."

Mom took a drink, levelling a stern look over the rim of her cup. "Seriously, while I'm gone, I want you doing homework and that's it. Okay?"

"I know," Mark said. "How long will you be gone?"

"Not very long."

Mark paused. "Like an hour?"

"Not long, Mark. It's none of your damn business. Just focus on getting your homework done."

Don't push it, or she'll get suspicious. Mark nodded. She wasn't going to budge. He rose from his chair and grabbed a bowl from the cupboard.

Mom gave him a half-smile as he discovered a box of Shreddies in the pantry. "I'm glad you're aware that breakfast is still permitted."

"Even prisoners get fed," Mark said.

"True," Mom said. "You're not in the execution chamber yet. Just don't ever land in that office again or *I* might have to kill you."

"I know, Mom."

He poured his cereal and sat at the table. Mom sipped her tea and picked up the paper where Dad had left it. Mark ate in silence, then rinsed his bowl and left the kitchen.

As he climbed the stairs to his room, Mom called from the kitchen. "I'm leaving, Mark. I want to see what you've been working on when I get back."

Mark stopped with a pang of anticipation, a pleasant lightness in his gut. He could do this; he felt it. He could spare a few minutes for the Shack.

"Okay, Mom," he called. "See you in a bit." He stood at the top of the stairs and listened until he heard the door close.

Now was his chance.

He made a discreet dash for his bedroom, fumbled into a pair of faded jeans, and waited for the sound of the garage door as he pulled a T-shirt over his head. This could work. He could make it work. If he kept his visit brief enough, there'd be no reason to get caught. Mom and Joanne always spent hours talking, anyway.

He could do this.

He finally heard the telltale sounds of the garage door closing and the crackle of gravel under tires.

He bolted down the stairs, missed a step in his excitement and tumbled the remainder of the way. His head clunked hard against the wall. It hurt like hell, but there was no time for hesitation; he collected himself, cursing and panting. He got his sneakers on, trying to control his shaking. Then, with a decisive nod, he opened the door and stepped outside.

The morning air was still cool despite the risen sun. He sprinted, avoiding the perturbed glance of a neighbour who was smoking on her porch. He ran the route that was now familiar, the chilly air fuelling his adrenaline.

So close, so close.

It's been too long.

His euphoria died when he arrived. The moment he reached the Shack's spot, his stomach cinched up and he became aware of his own thumping heart.

The Shack was gone.

What the fuck? This couldn't be. This was impossible. *How the fuck could it just disappear?* Mark whipped around, quickly becoming frantic. A building could not just vanish.

But it wasn't there. Everywhere he looked, there was nothing but grass. Bare grass.

His thoughts rushed through his mind in a frantic tumult, the phrase *What the fuck?* looping like an infectious song chorus. Somebody, some unspeakable thing, was toying with him. He tried briefly to tell himself that maybe this wasn't the right spot, but he quickly gave up. He knew very well that this was the place, and he knew that it was gone. He thought for a second that maybe some group of kids had burned it down, or that some concerned parent had called the local authorities, demanding that it be demolished—but there were no scorch marks on the ground, nor was there a patch of exposed soil or dead grass where the Shack had been.

A sound, sickened, slipped through Mark's lips. It frightened him a little, but only for the moment before hysteria set in. He ran, not sure why he was running. He ran until his calves were about to seize up. He collapsed on the ground, facedown. Blades of grass tickled his cheeks, bristled the insides of his nostrils.

The thought that this was a nightmare within a nightmare cartwheeled crazily across his mind.

He pressed his face into the ground and said, "This is a pillow and I am going to wake up. This is a dream." He began grinding his face harder into the soil. "Wake up." He ripped clumps of grass with his fingers. "Wake the fuck up right now."

He screamed and he hoisted himself to his knees, flecks of grass clinging to his flesh. His body lurched; a geyser of vomit surged up his throat and trickled into his mouth. He tasted the sourly sweet remnants of undigested Shreddies on their way back out, and he couldn't contain it any longer—yellow bile burst from his lips and hit the ground with an audible splat. The smell, like long-since-spoiled cream, made him nauseous again. He puked more, spewing pulped cereal across the grass.

"Fuck," he said. He doubled over. Gelatinous ropes swung from his lips; he coughed and spat them out. He thumped himself on the side of the head with his fists.

He heard a man shout in the distance. "Hey."

Mark jerked his head in the direction of the shout. Somewhere at the end of the field, a middle-aged man was walking down his driveway.

"Cut the screaming," the man yelled.

Mark rattled with fury as he rose to his feet. He stared at the nosy old prick with mounting rage. The guy was strutting toward the field, his khaki shorts scissoring.

"Fuck off." Mark said it to himself more than anyone.

Somehow, the man heard him, and began jogging at a steady clip. "What?"

Mark's good sense submitted to the pressure of rage. "Mind your own fucking business. Go back into your cozy fucking house before I kick your fucking eyeballs into your head."

His skin prickled, his stomach swam; he felt like an animal.

The man was advancing fast, but he was far enough away to allow Mark a decent head start. Nevertheless, Mark stood for a few more moments.

And he wished immediately that he hadn't.

For one petrifying moment, the man's face changed. There was no transition. One second Mark was looking at the sunburnt face of some angry man, and the next he was staring into the face of something else. Something inhumanly cruel. Something murderous.

And he knew instantly that it was the face from his dream—a face that probed from a mass of black clouds, taking the form of unthinkable horror. And as quickly as the change took place, Mark's nightmare re-emerged in his brain: brutal, vicious, all-consuming.

Mark screamed, falling backwards. The shrillness of his own voice startled him. The man-thing advanced, now at a full sprint. Catching up.

Mark was paralyzed before logic kicked in. This thing, whoever or whatever it was, would kill him if it caught up; it was as simple as that. He rose to his feet, turned around, and ran, ignoring the relentless burn that coursed through his legs. His guts bubbled and his body exploded with pain, but he didn't stop running until he arrived at his house.

He swung the door open, slammed it shut, and ran up the staircase, three steps at a time. He threw himself on his bed, and he shook and he cried. Mark was not the crying type, but he was sobbing now. He sobbed until urgent sickness worked back into his stomach. He stumbled into the bathroom, hunched over the toilet and gagged. There was nothing solid left inside him.

He coughed a fine mist of blood. Medical warning sign, bathroom dread. The sight alarmed him into momentary sense, and he collapsed beside the toilet, wheezing until he could breathe again.

The emptiness. The fucking emptiness. *How could this happen?* he thought. *How?*

Suddenly, the sound of Mom's voice jerked him to his feet. "Hey, I'm home."

How long had he been sitting here, panting beside the toilet? How long had he been in that empty field? Nothing made any sense. Somewhere in the background of his mind, he thought again that maybe this was all part of the same extended and hyper-real dream.

"Hi, Mom," he called. His voice didn't sound like his own. His throat was ravaged, his heart still rat-a-tatting.

He came to the frantic realization that he'd done no work since Mom had left. She might suspect something. She might know. He rushed to the sink and splashed water all over his face, then brushed his teeth. He ran to his room and unzipped his backpack, tossing some textbooks on the floor and displaying an open notebook on his desk. He sat in front of it, feigning intent focus.

Mom came into his room a few seconds later.

He glanced over his shoulder, trying to appear studious and undoubtedly failing. "Hi, Mom, how was your visit?"

Mom looked taken aback. He was overacting; he was being too polite. He became conscious again of his own rapid-fire heartbeat.

Mom approached, pausing a few feet behind him. "Fine, Mark," she said. "How is your homework coming along?"

"It's coming, I guess."

He expected her to kiss him on the head, or at least squeeze his shoulder—he expected *something*, but she didn't move any closer. Instead, she gave only a faint nod before walking back down the hall.

As soon as Mark heard her bedroom door closing, he began to hyperventilate. His stomach was bunching up, pinching globs of nonexistent fluid. His head tingled with lightness and he forced himself to catch his breath. He couldn't do this. He couldn't spend a week alone, not without the Shack. He could handle being away from his friends; that didn't really matter, but this…this was torture. The thought of losing the Shack made him feel cold and scared. So, so scared.

Chapter 10

MARK STARED AT THE NOTEBOOK ON his desk and imagined an opening sentence for the anti-violence essay that Weatherill had requested: *Violence is a very negative thing, especially if the guy whose teeth you're ripping out has just suffered the loss of a loved one…*

He massaged his temples and exhaled.

He couldn't remember the last time he'd written anything in this notebook, or in any of his notebooks, for that matter. His classes were a spaced-out blur. He almost always got away with simply pretending to look focused; by this point, his teachers left him alone as long as he didn't cause any disturbances. He was confident that he hadn't learned anything from school in his entire life. The only thing he'd learned from school was that he didn't belong in school.

He grabbed the notebook and moved over to his bed. He slipped into the sheets and laid sideways, vacant eyes fixed on the untouched page. He stayed that way until his eyelids took control, dimming his vision of those tedious loose-leaf lines. As exhaustion set in, he pushed the notebook aside. He made sure to leave it open, just in case Mom walked in and accused him of sleeping the day away.

He was nearly asleep when Mom called him to the kitchen. He jolted up, took a few groggy swipes at the blankets, and walked downstairs.

Mom was rinsing her hands in the sink. She glanced over her shoulder. "You look tired."

"Yeah."

She turned off the faucet and dried her hands on a dishtowel. She nodded toward a plate on the table. "I made you a sandwich."

Mark glanced at the plate, and his belly gurgled. He must've spouted every remainder of his stomach's contents, because he was famished.

"Thanks," he said.

"Yeah, well, like I said, you've still got to eat," Mom said.

"I know." He sat down and picked up the sandwich. Peanut butter and honey on white bread. "Thanks, Mom."

Mom hung the dishtowel on the oven handle. "You're welcome. I've got to do some paperwork now. Get back to your homework when you're done." She walked away. No hug, no kiss.

Mark bit into the sandwich. He ignored his body's pressure which, quite irrationally, tried to send the food back out. He held it down, drank some milk, and walked back up to his room. He sat at his desk and stared at his blank notebook with indifference. He shoved it aside, then picked up a social studies textbook from the floor.

As he cracked the book open, there was a loud and abrupt thump from behind. He jerked his head at the sound, expecting to see that his stand-up lamp had toppled onto the floor. Damn thing was getting old, and its foundation was wobbly.

He was puzzled to see, though, that the crooked lamp was still upright. He sat in silence for a moment, maintaining a level gaze and trying to think of possible sources for the noise. Maybe something had fallen over inside his closet? God knew it was a mess in there, and there were plenty of boxes that were defying gravity on the top shelf. Yes, something must've fallen. That must've been it.

He advanced toward the closet to pick up whatever had been dropped.

As he crossed the carpet, he heard the same sound again—not once, but twice. Consecutive thumps, like a hammer driving a nail. The volume and suddenness startled him; he retreated a step and gulped a scream that was fighting to get out. His chest tightened.

He went through the motions of reasoned self-talk. *There's nothing in the closet—how old are you? You're being paranoid. One thing falls over, bumps a couple other things, and then they fall over, too. Mystery solved.*

The self-talk would probably work if he could convince himself that it was true. But he knew something was in there, and he also knew that it was not just an old box of childhood toys.

"What do you want?" he said.

The sound of his own voice startled him so badly that he jumped. His shaking hand rose to his mouth and he pressed his palm to his lips, still holding that scream inside, trapping it in utero.

The thumping returned, big shuddering sounds between evenly timed pauses. How could Mom not hear this? It was getting louder and louder, sounding now like somebody was standing right behind the door, taking aggressive swings at the wall with a baseball bat. Or a sledgehammer.

Mark peeled his hand from his mouth, and he struggled to speak, struggled to react in some way.

The sound persisted, an impossible rise in volume.

"Stop," Mark said. "Just tell me. What do you want?"

Who…or what…*am I even talking to?*

Silence.

Mark tried to ward away the thoughts that goosefleshed his arms. He kept his eyes on the closet doors, waiting for the sound to come back. He sensed the presence of a follower. Sensed the lingering tension of pursuit.

The nightmare sensation again.

The thumping was finished; intuition told him so. Just as clearly as it told him that something was leaving the room.

Mark looked at his bedroom door and was overwhelmed by the impulse to run down to his mother.

He walked to the bathroom instead. He locked the door behind himself and sat on the toilet, trying not to look into the mirror. He didn't want to see his face.

But then he heard the noise, just one more thump, and he looked up in shock. He met his reflection and he cursed. He looked gaunt, too old to be true, eyes lit up with a terror he couldn't ignore. He jumped from the toilet and stood over the sink. He twisted the knob to the far right, all H and no C. When his reflection had been fully fogged out by the steam, he stuck his hands under the hot water. He held them under the stream until his flesh reddened, until pain set in. He inhaled between his teeth and withdrew his stinging fingers.

Something had begun.

***

Dad was still wearing his office clothes when he sat down for dinner. Navy blue jacket, navy blue pants. Subtly patterned shirt, buttons straining against the bulk of his abdomen.

He rubbed his fingertips into his eye sockets. "Hello there, Mark."

"Hi, Dad."

Mom set a bowl of potato soup in front of Mark. "Didn't have a fun day, did you?"

"No," Mark said.

Dad smiled thinly. "You lose your privileges when you misbehave." He turned to Mom. "Thanks, honey. The soup looks great."

Mom kissed him on the cheek. She sat down and said, "*Bon appetit*," and the family ate their soup in silence. As Mark scooped his final spoonful, Dad said, "I hope this is the last time you'll have to go through this."

"It will be, Dad."

Dad glanced down at Mark's hands, at the patches of crimson. The burns were already beginning to peel. Mark caught Dad's glance and set his palms down on his lap. Dad sniffed deeply, and Mark could see that he was restraining a smile.

Later that evening, as Mark submerged his hands in dishwater, he grimaced at the discomfort. Although the burns hurt, and although they reminded him of things better left unremembered, he told himself that he'd just been overexcited, that things would soon clear up. *Soon, everything will be good again*, he thought as he towel-dried the dishes; whenever he left the dishes to drip-dry in the drying rack, Dad asked him if he only had half an ass—when Mark invariably said "no," Dad said, "Well then don't do a half-assed job on the dishes." The joke didn't make much sense to Mark, but he'd never tell that to Dad.

Mom and Dad were sitting in the living room, watching a talk show interview with a bestselling American writer; the writer was saying that nobody ever asked him about his use of language.

"Ha," Dad said at the screen. "Poor rich guy, right? Boo-hoo, right?"

"Shh," Mom said, swatting his beefy chest playfully.

Mark stood on the outskirts of the room for a moment before Mom glanced at him. Usually she asked him if he wanted to watch television with them.

Not tonight, though.

"Well, I'm going to bed," Mark said.

"Okay, good night. I love you," Mom said, then turned back to the screen.

"Night," Dad said without turning at all. "Love you, buddy."

Mark nodded and walked up to his bedroom.

Lying in bed that night, he couldn't stop staring at the closet, his wide eyes delving into darkness, his body translating ugly thoughts into sickness and shakes, an awful feeling like sexual arousal mixed with terror. He sensed the Shack, making its presence known.

In that queasy, quivering space of time, the truth arrived: he had to go back there. He couldn't be certain that the Shack was gone for sure. He allowed himself the thought that maybe, somehow, he'd been deceived by his own senses.

Or maybe something else was deceiving him. Maybe the Shack was making itself unseen.

He shuddered and pulled the blankets up to his chin. Curled into the fetal position, like a child hiding from ghosts.

The thought of visiting the Shack didn't excite him this time, no, that wasn't it, but still… none of the intensity was gone. He still quivered uncontrollably, impulse still pinned his thoughts into corners. But he knew it was a different kind of visit this time; he couldn't risk going alone, not after seeing that nightmare shape charge at him.

He would need his friends.

Wide-eyed, balled up under his blankets, he noted that the closest phone was downstairs. Not only would he have to sneak out the door, he would have to sneak in the quiet phone calls, too.

He could feel the Shack pulling, stronger than last time. He glanced at the bold red digits on his alarm clock: 10:30. Too early still.

He pulled the blanket further, covering his head; he compressed his body and tried to let his mind wander. His thoughts drifted suddenly, unexpectedly, to Madeline. He thought about the countless smiles they'd exchanged; he tried to quantify them with a specific number. It was not the first smile that he remembered most vividly, but perhaps the seventh or the ninth or the twelfth, when her smile first seemed to be graced with the invisible accompaniment of something else, when he thought that maybe the smile was not just a smile. How many times had they exchanged a glance without exchanging names? How many opportunities had he gotten to speak with her? How many had we wasted? He pushed the thoughts aside as well as he could. Thought about her eyes and how her hair looked when she tied it back. Thought about her body.

Madeline Fraley.

The presence of gray, peeling walls rose from his unconscious to take shape in his consciousness again. He couldn't avoid it for long.

For a fleeting moment, he realized that Madeline had made the Shack go away…away from his mind, at least. Even from an unknowable distance, she'd pushed it from his thoughts.

Time was invisible under the blanket. He stayed submerged for as long as he could, safe, soft, and enclosed. Infinity filled an hour. He emerged from the covers, blinking in fear at the blackness, and he looked at the clock again: 11:23.

Close enough.

He studied the closet as he rose from his bed, and he kept his eyes on it while he crossed the room, like watching a predator that might leap at any moment. He descended the stairs with caution, glancing at his parents' room to make sure their door was closed.

He made it to the nearest phone.

He gulped anxiously at the beeping of the buttons as he dialed Adam's number; listening to the dial tone, he was overtaken by the horrifying realization that Adam's dad might pick up. If Adam's dad was suffering from a bad enough wine headache, he might be very, very unfriendly. He might just take out his frustration on Adam, or his wife, or both of them; he might sit them down in the living room and scream in their faces, might squeeze his wife's breasts in front of Adam and ask Adam when he'd find a love-toy for himself.

He'd done it before. Mark had seen it.

After three rings, Mark heard the click of someone picking up. He tensed, waited for the greeting.

"Hello?" It was Adam's brother, the unseen man himself, the provider of cigarettes, the enigmatic badass.

"Hey," Mark said, his heart slowing noticeably. "Is Adam home?"

"Uh, yeah, I think he's gaming," Adam's brother replied. "One sec."

Mark heard the ruffling of movement, then static and distant exchanges before a moment of tentative silence, and then finally, Adam asking, "Who's this?"

Mark didn't know if he'd ever been so relieved to hear his angry and unpredictable friend's voice.

"Adam, it's Mark," he said. "You're going to think this is fucked up, but we have to go to the Shack."

Adam gave a sigh, transmitted to a crackle of static through the phone. "Are you serious?"

"As cancer."

Adam sighed another crackly sigh. "When?"

"Tonight."

Adam groaned. "Didn't you get yourself expelled or something, man?"

"No," Mark said. "I got suspended. We can talk about it later."

"I heard you were still fuckin' around with Clinton."

Mark slapped himself on the forehead. *Can't you just shut up and listen for one minute?*

He thought he heard a door open and he pressed the phone's mouthpiece to his chest. He craned his neck toward the staircase, waited several seconds. When he'd determined that it was only his imagination, he brought the phone back to his ear.

"We can talk about it later," he said.

"What's been up with you? What is it with this place, this Shack thing?" Adam asked.

"Look, I don't know, all right? Can you just do me this favour?"

Adam groaned again, but Mark suspected that he'd roped him in.

"Is Scott coming or what?" Adam asked.

Adam's in. He would've hung up by now if he wasn't, Mark thought. "I hope Scott's coming too, yeah. We'll have to go to his place. I don't want to risk calling him."

"So what are you saying?" Adam's voice rose. "It's all right to risk my dad crackin' my head open, but Scott can't handle a little fucking reprimand? Huh?"

Mark paused. Before dialling, he hadn't even considered the risk for Adam.

"What the fuck, man?" Adam yelled.

"Scott's folks hate me," Mark said coolly. "They'd tell my parents, and then I'd be screwed."

"Right. So it's about you."

Mark's jaw tensed and he had the brief urge to throw the phone against the wall. Instead, he held it to his chest. Dad had always told him to count to ten when he got angry. So he counted to ten.

"No," he said when he'd finished the count. "It's not about me."

Silence.

"I'm sorry," he added.

The magic words. "Give me a few minutes to get ready," Adam said. "You coming here?"

"Yeah, I think I'll walk over," Mark said. "It'll take a while."

"Okay, see you in a bit."

As Mark set down the phone, he asked himself what he'd do if the Shack still wasn't there. What if it really was gone?

Adam and Scott would assume it'd been taken down.

By who? They'd have an answer.

Why? They'd have an answer.

But Mark kept getting the feeling that this wasn't something that could be answered.

The eagerness and excitement he used to feel about the Shack was now an indistinct shape in his memory. He tried to push his fear away, but it wouldn't leave; he'd seen that face, a face made of clouds…he'd seen the leering shape of something that wanted to hurt him.

He stood in the darkness for a moment, eyes closed; then, with an absent nod, he walked to the front door and got into his shoes. Forbidding himself the chance to give it another thought, he walked out into the night.

It was cold again tonight. Cold every night.

He started running, a forced effort to warm his blood.

It seemed like it took half the night to get to Adam's house. He ran as often as he could, sometimes slowing to a walk. He'd never been the athletic type, but lately it seemed like he never stopped running.

When Mark arrived, he saw Adam standing outside. Adam's eyes flickered under a hood. He looked like a frightened cat cornered by a pissed-off Rottweiler.

"Are you all right?" Mark asked.

"You scared the shit out of me on the phone," Adam said.

"Sorry," Mark said. "I need your help."

Adam spat into the neighbor's shrubs. "Well, are you going to tell me what the fuck's going on or what?"

"Later. Let's go get Scott."

Adam exhaled harshly, and they started walking, their breath fogging. Adam turned to look at him as they moved. "You didn't tell me why you got suspended."

"Clinton came at me again," Mark said. "I wasn't going to say sorry a second time."

"You never said sorry to begin with."

"Yes I did."

Adam gave him a cocked smile. "Whatever. I bet like fuck that you didn't say it like you meant it."

"It doesn't matter," Mark said. "I learned my lesson the first time. The kid nearly broke my ribs."

"So, what, did you beat the shit out of him?"

"No. I got a few punches in, but Corr pulled me off before the fight really got going," Mark said. He remembered Clinton's tooth glinting in a nervy red lump on the grass. *Never really got going, huh?* "It was quick."

Adam coughed into his fist. "Goddamn. What if your parents find out you're sneaking around like this tonight? Is it really worth it over that stupid fucking shack?"

"I don't have a choice," Mark said.

Adam must've heard conviction in Mark's response, because he didn't ask any more questions.

When they finally reached Scott's house, Mark turned to his friend. "All right, Adam," he said. "Go knock on his window. I'll wait somewhere out of sight."

"What? Why me? You fuckin' do it."

Don't snap back. Just take it easy. If you explain yourself right, you'll get through to him.

"I can't risk it," Mark said, his voice level. "Scott's parents know what your dad is like. They'll think you just want to hide out or something. But if they so much as *sense* me, they'll think the three of us are up to something suspicious."

Mark felt a little ashamed as he spoke. He knew that he was using his friends, and he had the genuine fear that they were all about to do something very dangerous.

Adam made a strange and nearly inaudible sound, almost like a whimper.

"I'm sorry to do this. I mean it," Mark said.

Adam waved the apology away. "Go hide. Wait around the corner of the cul-de-sac and we'll come get you."

Mark patted him on the shoulder and ran off. Waiting outside the cul-de-sac, he looked up at the sky: blackness marbled with dark blue. He focused on his inhalation and exhalation, an absurd attempt to blot out the quiet, to stay sane.

In less than a minute, Scott and Adam came running toward him, hunched like soldiers ducking gunfire. They peered at him from under their hoods, expressing mutual terror with their half-shielded eyes.

"You're not going to tell me what the hell is going on, are you?" Scott asked.

Adam looked frightened, no doubt, but Scott looked like he'd just had a conversation with a convicted serial killer. He scratched his thighs with his fingertips, casting twitchy glances into the darkness.

"We're going to the Shack," Mark said.

Scott scratched harder, and Mark's skin tingled from the sound of flesh scraping denim.

"Why?" Scott asked.

Mark smiled humorlessly. "Like you said, I'm not going to tell you what the hell is going on."

Scott turned to look at Adam.

"I don't know what's up, either, man," Adam said.

They stood on the shadow-painted sidewalk for a minute, hushed.

Mark's nerves committed assault on his patience. "Let's get going."

And so they walked. Scott kept peering over his shoulder and alternating glances of caution from Mark to Adam.

"You got suspended, didn't you, Mark?" Scott asked. His voice sounded severe, even disapproving.

Fear gnawed through Mark's thoughts. The question agitated him. Who the hell cared about his suspension? He answered nevertheless. "Yeah, I did."

"Jesus, Mark," Scott said. "Suspension. That's serious."

"Yeah, I know."

"I mean, you should really watch yourself, you know," Scott pressed. "You got *suspended*."

Mark hesitated. "Yes. I got suspended."

Scott opened his mouth to say something else, but he closed the words back inside. After a reluctant minute, he continued. "Mark, I heard you ripped his tooth out. I mean, they don't just suspend you for nothing."

"It's been pretty well fucking established, Scott," Mark said. "Yes, I got suspended. I bashed Clinton's head until he cried like the baby that he is. He tried pushing me around and he got what he deserved. Are the two of you done with the suspension crap yet?"

"Chill the fuck out. We didn't have to sneak out for you tonight," Adam said.

Mark didn't reply. As they walked, he felt more and more like he was marching to an execution. By the time they reached the edge of the field, he suspected that it must be close to three in the morning. He turned to his friends and looked hard at both of them.

"This is going to sound corny, but I don't care," he said. "Whatever happens tonight, we stick together. It's very important that I tell you this, because I don't know what we might bump up against."

"You need to tell me just what the fuck is going on, Mark," Scott said, his voice quaking.

"I wish I knew what the fuck is going on, Scott," Mark replied.

Adam bounced on his feet, like a boxer in the corner of the ring. "Let's do this fuckin' thing."

Scott made a visible attempt to get himself together, but his eyes were still crazed with fear. The trio walked together, Mark flagged by his hooded friends.

As they walked into the field, Mark's eyes met the thing that terrified him the most: even more terrifying than the possibility of absence…the confirmation of renewed presence. Gray walls of unknown material and obscure memories. Shapeless structure, shapeless purpose. The Shack. His mind shrieked with nightmare flashbacks. His stomach felt like it was practicing for *Cirque du Soleil.*

He wanted to say something to his buddies, to confess his discovery of the Shack's disappearance, or to suggest turning around, but his mouth was sealed and his body wouldn't stop moving.

If the Shack had still been gone tonight, he could've talked and reasoned away its disappearance; it might not have been easy to do, but he could've found some explanation. Yes, with the help of his friends, he could've produced an answer, and with an explanation could've come the possibility of forgetting, of moving forward. He imagined he could've become a satisfactory student and finally asked Madeline Fraley for her phone number, or if she would like to go out on a date with him, and he could've regained his parents' trust, and he could've started, finally, to feel normal.

Now, the physical actuality of the Shack seemed to confirm that he couldn't have any of those things.

He could hear Scott's breath, puffing out more and more raggedly as they advanced.

"Oh fuck oh fuck oh God I really don't want to do this please please," Scott was murmuring, tears pushing through his words.

They were now within a meter of the Shack, and Mark sensed something impending, danger like he'd never known. He looked at Scott, whose eyes were still shifting in all directions.

"Scott," he said. "If you don't want to do this, you can leave now. I won't judge you."

A pause. Scott still mumbling to himself.

"You too, Adam. I can do this alone. I realized that just now. I thought before that I would need somebody here, but now I know that I have to go in there. No matter what. Whatever you two decide, I'm still going in."

"I didn't sneak out for nothing, man. It's just a stupid fucking shack. I'm ready when you are," Adam said.

Mark nodded at him and turned to Scott again. "Scott?"

Scott pulled his hood down over his eyes, hunched over. He maintained that unsettling pose for a while, then began rocking on his heels. Scott was whispering, and Mark couldn't make out his words for a moment, but the cadences were familiar: Scott was reciting *Hail Mary*. After finishing, he pulled himself upright, removed his hood, and wiped his eyes.

"I'm going in," he said.

The final confirmation. Mark slipped his finger into the crack of the door. Terror resurrected by physical contact with the Shack. It was undeniably tangible. Undeniably real.

He pulled the door open and stepped inside; the smell was warm and rustic, wafting in invisible currents from the cracking walls. The aroma was powerfully reassuring. Whatever horror he'd been feeling was already passing away. He closed his eyes and drew it in through his nostrils, taking in this place's stories. Letting them flow into him.

"Mark?"

Mark opened his eyes, allowing his pupils to adjust. He wasn't certain who'd said his name, but he responded anyway. "Yes?"

"What do we do now?" Adam asked. "Why are we here?"

Mark could hear the aggravation in Adam's voice, but his own fear continued waning, replaced by that irreplaceable sense of safety that only the Shack could bring. Nothing was wrong; how could it be? Maybe he'd imagined the whole disappearance. Yes, he must have. It seemed unbelievable, but even more unbelievable was the possibility that the entire thing had just vanished. Things didn't just disappear. That was ridiculous. His senses must've deceived him.

"Yeah, Mark," Scott said. "Can you fill us in? What's this about?"

Their voices were fading into the background, washing under a wave of ancient chronicles. The Shack's timeless and secret narratives crushing their words.

"If you're just going to fucking stand there without doing anything, I'm getting the fuck out of here before my parents wake up," Adam said. "I'd rather not get two black eyes from my dad this morning." He started to turn away, but Scott's eyes were still fixed on Mark's back. Adam stopped at the door, wheeled around and looked at Scott. "Scott? Are you coming with me?"

"I don't know, Adam," Scott said. "I'm scared. What if something happens?"

"What the fuck could happen? It's a fucking shack. It's an old, run-down piece of shit and Mark has a hard-on for it, for some goddamn reason. I don't want to get my ass kicked over this," Adam said. His voice boomed in the small space, trapped in its colorless confines.

"Then leave," Mark said.

Adam advanced on him, gripped him hard by the arm. "Mark, wake up. Jesus, what is going on with you? Huh? Are you even listening to me, for Christ's sake? What is it with this fucking pl—"

A thump.

All three of them jerked their heads simultaneously. The sound had come from upstairs. Adam's fingers dug deeper into Mark's flesh.

Mark kept his gaze fixed upward. "I'm going up there."

The thumping continued.

"Mark. What is that?" Scott asked, his voice somewhere far away. "Mark, what is that horrible *sound*?"

"I don't know," Mark said. "Go ahead. Leave."

Adam shook Mark by the shoulders. "What the fuck is wrong with you? We're not going anywhere. What if there's some psycho up there, huh? Jesus, Mark. What are we going to do then? It's like you've never seen a fuckin' horror movie before."

The thumping persisted, built into a rhythmic frequency, like a metronome.

Or a funeral drum.

Mark advanced to the staircase. Scott, crying, a dry huffing sound in the periphery of his mind.

It sounds just like a heartbeat.

The stairs sagged under their feet, less wood than rot. Mark moved faster as he neared the top. This was what he'd been waiting for; this was where he wanted to be.

The harsh, coronary thumping was now violently loud. Mark's teeth rattled. He raised a foot onto the top floor, quivering with excitement. He stepped onto it and, with one final thump, the sound stopped. Adam and Scott jogged up to meet him.

Scott grabbed Mark's wrist and Mark pulled away.

"Yes. This is it," Mark said. He wasn't sure he could explain what he meant, but the words sounded right.

There was a narrow hall at the top of the stairs, lined with a half-decayed banister; it led to a single room. The door was closed.

"We're not going in there, Mark," Scott said. "Think about this. What if somebody's in there? We could get killed. Or worse."

"He's right, we should leave," Adam said, his voice low and steady: a desperate, unusual attempt at reason.

Mark ignored them and started down the hall, one hand caressing the desiccated banister. He reached the door and touched it with his fingertips. Massaged it. "Yes. This is it."

"This is what? This is fucking what?" Adam said.

Mark gently pushed the warped, blackish wood, and it eased open. The room gaped at them like a gigantic mouth. Impenetrable darkness. Mark entered. His eyes wouldn't adjust to this blackness; it was unlike anything he'd experienced. Darker than darkness. Total, all-consuming mystery crushed between four ageless walls.

Adam and Scott crept in behind him.

"Mark, I can't see," Scott said. "Oh my god I can't see oh Jesus Mark please I can't see a thing."

A thump, impossibly close this time. It sounded like somebody clapping two hardcover books by Mark's ears. Scott screamed, and the door swung closed.

"Who's in here? What the fuck do you want?" Adam snapped.

"Oh please don't hurt us oh god oh god oh god oh god."

"Show your fucking face, you psycho."

"This can't be happening Mark please please please get us out of here please."

The sound rotated around the room, like a tremendous spider doing laps along the walls; it circled and circled, blackening their collective sense of reason, until finally, after a minute or an hour or four hours…it halted again. There was a millisecond of dark silence, then the room burst into light. Not a warm, natural light, but a white blast, a ghostly explosion of rays. And standing in the center of the room, Mark saw it.

The nightmare shape of featureless features. Malice staring through fog. And now he was close enough to make out its appearance in terrifying detail: limbs too long to be human, pale purplish flesh pulled taut over its bones—like the skin of a decaying junkie. Tattered fabric dangled from its shoulders and legs, holes revealing its grotesquely emaciated form. But no matter how hard Mark tried to see its face, he couldn't make out anything through that oily black cloud—a thick and broiling form that blotted out its features.

Somewhere in his mind, Mark knew that his friends were screaming. Somewhere else in his mind, he knew that urine was pooling in his underwear and trickling down the insides of his thighs.

The shape moved, arms dangling like discarded goods. It actually *moved* toward Mark, taking slow and deliberate steps, an evil smear gliding in the whiteness. It stood an inch in front of him, and he could smell them again, those stories, stronger than ever, but they weren't alluring or seductive; no, now they smelled sour.

Mark's mind leapt crazily to a childhood memory, when he'd walked into the storage room of his parents' undeveloped basement to investigate the source of a pungent odour; he'd pulled the light bulb cord, revealing a dead mouse inches in front of him, expired and mortified on the marmalade shelf. The mouse was shrivelled into a grotesque brown circle, putrefying claws curled on its matted chest. Ants were crawling over its flesh, and Mark had seen one slip between its pointed teeth. The stench now crushing his senses was something like the smell of that rotting mouse, but much more potent.

He stared straight into the fog, his heart coming close to palpitations. The thing drilled its gazeless gaze into him. It could do anything it wanted. It could kill him.

But it didn't.

Instead it moved past him, swimming through the paranormal blankness toward his friends. Their cries intensified, and the light cut out. The room was encompassed in dark blindness again.

Mark was now acutely aware of the hideous, ballistic shrieks that his friends were emitting in the corner. His panic rose and he swung around, his arms swiping at the unknown. "Stop, stop. Enough."

There was an airy sucking sound, like a giant vacuum hose swallowing dust, and then, abruptly, finally, the door clapped open.

Mark saw a hazy silhouette in the corner rise up and become Adam, who bolted out the doorway. Mark ran after him. They clattered into the hallway, hyperventilating.

"Where's Scott?" Adam asked immediately.

Mark spun, a mad look in his eyes. He couldn't see Scott either. Nowhere.

"I don't know."

Adam's face contorted into a mask of fury. He seized Mark's throat. "What the fuck do you mean, you don't know? He was just in there. We have to go get him."

Mark wanted to go in there and rescue his friend, but somehow he already knew the truth: the Shack had taken Scott. It could have taken Mark, and it could've taken Adam, but it took Scott instead. He stared into Adam's frantic eyes, barely even aware of the fingers clutching at his esophagus.

"He's gone," he rasped, his voice depleting.

Adam released his hold, but his eyes were still panicked. "How do you know?"

"I just know."

For the moment, Adam needed no further explanation. They ran down the stairs and out the door. As they broke outside, Mark glanced toward the houses in the distance; he looked at the house from which he'd first seen the nightmare shape emerge.

The man-thing was standing upright on the front step, arms hanging at its sides, eyes shifting in a face like pixels, a face without definition. A face that channeled its own image of hell from a distance. It stared at Mark, unmoving. Then, in an eerily smooth gesture, it raised a thin finger, extending its arm to point at him. Even from this distance, he could feel the thing.

"Adam, we're not safe yet."

"What?"

"Run."

"My lungs are going to collapse."

"Fucking run."

They did just that: fucking ran all the way to Adam's house. The sun was rising, a golden tint probing at the blackness.

Adam's hands violently rattled as he fumbled with the doorknob. They rushed inside, kicking their shoes off with all the discretion they could muster, and they made their way to Adam's room.

Shaking, Adam took a seat on the edge of his bed. Mark sat beside him.

"Mark... What the fuck was that?"

"I don't know." Mark's voice was incapable, miniscule.

Adam looked at him, a crazed expression. "Don't fuck with me. You brought us there. What happened? Where's Scott?"

Fear, much like a trigger, set off Mark's anger. He couldn't handle Adam's irrational demand for explanations. Not now. Not when his mind felt so much like a widening crevice, open to all the sinister capacities of madness.

"I don't know," he said again.

"Where is Scott?" Adam repeated, now shouting.

Indignation manifested as a stab in Mark's temple, as powerful as it was sudden; he clenched a handful of Adam's shirt and swung him toward the floor, where Adam's head connected with a blunt thud.

Mark lowered his face to Adam's. "If you have any fucking sense, you won't continue screaming your head off like that."

Adam's eyes slanted, threatening violence.

Mark raised his fist over Adam's face and let it hover in the air. "Be smart, Adam."

The anger dissipated from Adam's face until he looked small, defeated, and embarrassed. Mark released him, and Adam crumpled in a heap, slack and unmoving.

Mark towered over him and gathered his thoughts; then, choosing his words with meticulous care, he spoke. "We can't tell a single person what happened tonight. This is more important than anything. We have to make that promise to each other right now, that no matter what happens, we cannot say a word about this."

Adam rose to a sitting position. "You can't be serious."

"Believe me, I am. Not a word."

"What if they can help us find Scott? What, are we just going to leave him?"

"Who's going to help us?"

"The police, or maybe—"

"Scott is gone, and you know it. I have no clue where he is, but wherever it is, he's never coming back. Accept it. Accept it now."

Don't ask me how I know, but I do. Somehow I just do.

"I can't. That's fucking insane, Mark. Where is he?"

"We don't know." Mark allowed his words a moment to set in. "Accept it and move on."

"Mark, this is so fucking crazy."

Mark paced back and forth across the room, clenching and unclenching his fists, carving deep fingernail indents in his palms. He stopped and sat again on the edge of Adam's bed, hiding his face in his hands.

He could hardly believe he was saying what he was saying, but he was even more terrified by how *sure* he was.

"Mark… Mark, this is fucking crazy."

Mark dropped his hands on his lap and looked Adam in the eyes. "I know this is crazy. That's what I'm trying to say. If you tell anybody that you saw Scott disappear, *kapoof*, in a shack in the middle of the suburbs, what do you think they're going to say to you?"

"Maybe if we explained everything…"

Mark continued staring into Adam's frantic face. "Let me tell you what'll happen if you try to 'explain everything.' They're going to say that you probably got at your dad's Stephen King collection as a young child. That's what they're going to say. And at first they're going to laugh about it, sure, until they find out that Scott's actually gone. Because people will find out, Adam, and that's when they're going to start getting suspicious. That's when they're going to find out that you were involved and that's when they're going to throw you into juvenile hall."

"But I wasn't involved. He fucking disappeared," Adam exploded.

Mark's fury, an undertow, broke dangerously close to the surface; he rose from the bed for a moment, then sat back down.

Like Dad always said: count to ten.

"What did I just tell you?" Mark said. "If you yell again, I'll give you a concussion."

Adam closed his eyes and drew in a slow, shaky inhale of air. He took a few moments to gather his thoughts. "They can't throw me in juvy hall, Mark. They don't have proof of anything. What can they possibly accuse me of?"

"Murder."

Adam barked a single laugh. "Murder. What the fuck are you talking about?"

"I'm trying to get this through your head. The police don't believe in the unknown, all right? Only the known. If we tell them that Scott was with us tonight, they're going to get ideas based on what they know. If they look into our histories, they'll see that your dad's been thrown in the drunk tank six thousand times. That's evidence enough for the police to pin you as a problem child. And I've been in enough fights to be labelled the same way. If we say anything about tonight, we can both consider ourselves fucked. Plain and simple."

Adam clutched at his hair, bunched it up in his hands and squeezed. His breath came out audibly, rapidly.

"I know this is hard," Mark said. "We're going to have to figure something out for ourselves. But before anything happens, I need you to make this promise."

Adam pressed fists against his eyes, unmoving on the floor. Mark's agitation continued mounting, until that familiar heat buzzed in his pores, wiping logic away. He counted to ten yet again, an attempt to stay steady.

"Don't fuck with me on this, Adam," he said. "Make this promise and we can figure it out from there. But nothing happens until you make the promise."

Adam nodded, his eyes still covered.

"What does that mean? That nod. What does it mean?" Mark said.

"I promise."

Mark's temper faded, little by little, and he opened his hands, glancing at the divots he'd made in the flesh. He looked at Adam's alarm clock. It was past five in the morning.

"I have to go," he said. "If I'm not home this morning, my parents will catch on."

"Catch on to what?"

Have you not listened to a single word I've said this entire time?

"The fact that we were involved. The fact that we were with Scott when he disappeared."

Adam's face whitened, terror flicking in his eyes.

Is it sinking in yet, you fucking idiot?

"Meet me tomorrow night and we can talk this over," Mark said. "I need to leave."

Sitting on the floor, Adam looked up at Mark, wide-eyed, imploring. Mark gave a curt nod and left the room. He yanked on his shoes and found himself running yet again, uncomforted by the honey glow of early morning. When he arrived home, he slipped through the door like a specter. Nobody was awake as he slid into bed. He fixed his eyes on the closet, from which he'd first heard that horrible thumping sound.

He didn't even consider the possibility of sleep.

Chapter 11

THE PHONE RANG EARLY, NOT LONG after Mark had slipped through the door.

Mom picked it up in her bedroom, and Mark heard her talking. The implications of the conversation were immediately clear to him.

"Hello?" she said. A brief pause. "No. No, I don't think so. Mark has been home all week." A longer pause. "Oh my God. He didn't say anything. Maybe he just… Let me go talk to him. He's still in bed. Just one moment. Okay. I know."

Mark closed his eyes at the sound of his parents' bedroom door. He rolled over and pretended to sleep.

Knuckles tapped on his door.

"Come in," he said, using his best imitation of a waking grumble.

Mom entered the room and gave him a concerned look. "You didn't go out last night, did you?"

Mark's adrenaline spiked. He kept his face hidden behind his pillows, still turned toward the wall. "No, of course not," he said.

Mom sighed and began walking back toward the door.

Mark rolled over and propped himself up, resting his back against the wall. "Why, Mom?"

Mom rotated her ring, staring at a spot on the carpet. "Scott's father is on the phone. Apparently he can't find Scott."

And he's not going to find Scott. Because Scott's not coming back.

Mark tried not to shudder. He furrowed his brow. "That's strange. Maybe Scott went somewhere."

Mom nudged a pile of dirty laundry aside with her foot, sifting through Mark's room with her eyes. "Well, apparently he called Adam's place and Scott's not there, either."

Mark and Mom made eye contact, and he could see that she was prodding at him. Beginning to calculate.

She doesn't know anything, so just calm down, she can't do anything because she doesn't know anything.

He shrugged. "Maybe he just went to get snacks or something. Scott's dad is always over-monitoring him."

Mom didn't look convinced. "I think it would be too early for him to go out and do *anything*, Mark."

Mark realized he hadn't even glanced at his clock since he'd made it home. "What time is it?"

"It's 6:30 in the morning," Mom said.

"How does his dad even know he's not there already?"

"What do you mean?"

Mark paused, processing the question or multiple questions he'd unwittingly posed. "Well, I doubt Scott is normally out of bed at 6:30."

"Apparently he left his bedroom door open and he wasn't in there," Mom said. "His dad looked all over the house and he couldn't find him anywhere."

Mark could not help but think, *Why the earthly fuck did Scott leave his door open?*

"I'm sure he'll turn up," he said, and slid back into his sheets.

"I hope so."

Mom left, shutting the door softly behind her. As she padded down the hall, Mark heard the subtlest thump from the inside of his closet. Quiet, but unmistakable. He rose to a sitting position, then shrunk back as he heard the thump again. He burrowed into the blankets, pulling them tight over his head.

He had the strange sensation that he'd just broken free from the chokehold of an otherworldly, malevolent dream, only to drift off into a darker and even more powerful one. He pressed down into his pillow, pulled the fabric taut over his face. He screamed, sucking cotton, a sound muted by whiteness.

***

The phone rang again at about four, and Mark answered.

It was Adam.

"Hey," Mark said. He craned his neck to see if his parents were nearby and noted that, mercifully, they were nowhere to be seen.

"Did Scott's dad call you today?" Adam asked.

Mark took a second, cautionary glance. "Yeah."

"This is for real, isn't it?"

"Yes, this is for real."

Mark could hear Adam attempting to control his inhalation: a series of static-crackled streams.

"Let's meet up tonight," Mark said. "You know that convenience store we always used to go to?"

Another rush of Adam's breath, fuzzy and electric. "Yeah, of course."

"Meet me there," Mark said. "Half past midnight."

Adam's silent response seemed, to Mark, like the moments before complete hysteria.

"Adam?"

"Yeah. Okay, half past midnight," Adam said finally.

Dinner came: the daily space for interrogation. It was only a few minutes before Mom raised the issue of Scott, and Dad scrutinized Mark with a stare.

"Mark, what happened to Scott?" Mom asked bluntly.

"How should I know? I've been home all week."

"Hey, watch the lip, buddy. Don't be rude," Dad said.

"I don't know where he is, Dad." Mark met Dad's eyes. "I'm worried."

Dad took a drink of milk, visibly softened. He hesitated, then said, "Now, I know I'm always asking, but I keep thinking that Scott is Adam. Which one is Scott again?"

Mark found himself unable to describe Scott. He looked at his plateful of overcooked meat, starch, and wet vegetables.

Say something. Answer him.

"He's the quiet one," he managed. "Kind of keeps to himself. Doesn't usually say much."

Dad scrunched up his eyebrows and nodded. It was clear he still had no clue who the fuck Mark was talking about.

There were no more questions. Not for now, at least.

Mom ate, visibly in thought; she refrained from comment.

***

Later, as he lay in bed, Mark's thoughts circled back to Mom's silence; fear, sharp, a coiling of the guts. *Does she know? Even if she knows* something, *she can't possibly know* everything…

His bleary gaze alternated between the closet and the alarm clock. No ominous sounds greeted him tonight, and 11 pm arrived after a torturous wait. Numb and blank-minded, he exited his house and stepped into the black street. Tonight, he had no impulse to run.

Adam was not yet at the convenience store when Mark arrived.

Mark looked through the window and watched uniformed clerks chattering behind the counter, their conversations muted by the glass. Mark paced the perimeter of white fluorescence shining from the window.

He heard a man's voice from the outskirts of the light: "Hey, you. Hey, man."

The voice was hoarse, desperate, maybe doped up.

Mark squinted in the direction of the voice and saw a man slouched against the wall, head tilted upward, a baseball cap shading his face. His knees were pulled close to his chest, arms folded across. Hands dangling, dirty.

Turn him down for money and look away. The last thing you need is trouble.

"Hey," Mark said.

"Hey, kid, listen, I've got a problem," the man said. "Maybe you can help me."

Every message from Mark's upbringing told him he should be frightened: he remembered hazy analog images from videos shown in kindergarten class, close-ups of faintly smiling men saying, "Don't talk to strangers." He remembered Mom telling him to always bring a pal when he walked to the convenience store, she called it the buddy system, and she echoed the video messages: "Don't talk to strangers."

Mark observed the man's unclear shape with indifference. He waited.

"Can you help me," the man said again, making it sound less like a question this time.

"I don't know."

The man huffed, wheezed, and coughed. "I know it sounds like bullshit but look…" He wiped his face with a dirt-caked hand. He pulled up his pant leg, revealing fresh scar tissue glistening on his shin. Bone poking through, pinkish fluid reflecting dim light.

"I fell asleep earlier and this happened," the man said. "I'm sick and I don't have a place to stay. I passed out in that alley over there and while I was out these kids poured lighter fluid all over my leg and they set it on fire. One of them was recording it on a camcorder. I couldn't even chase after them because I was just rolling around, you know, trying to put the flames out. They just kept laughing and laughing."

Mark stared at the man.

"They said they wanted to put the video on YouTube," the man said. "I heard them say that as they ran away."

Mark said nothing.

"It hurts so bad, man. Looks infected, too, and I can't…I can't—"

"You can't what?"

"Look, can you help me?"

"I told you I don't know."

The man showed no sign that he'd heard Mark speak. He held his hands in front of his face, palms out.

"Okay, well listen, my buddy says he's gonna pick me up tonight, right? Then he doesn't show up and I'm new to town here and this is what happens. A bunch of punks use me for their little *Jackass* video. This is what happens. Now I'm stuck out here and I don't know where the hell I'm going. I just need a little bit of money for a bus. Can you help me?"

"Busses don't run this late," Mark said, and knew it to be true.

Wheezing. Coughing. "They run all night." The gathering of nasal backup, the splat of mucus on pavement.

"Not in this neighborhood."

The man shook his head and laughed joylessly to himself. "Well damn. Do you have enough money for a taxi or something? I hate to ask, only this leg looks really bad and I don't know where I am, man. I should get my leg looked at, you know?"

"Call an ambulance."

"Come on, man." The man hacked. "Just a few bucks."

"No."

The man dropped his hands to his sides. "What?"

"No," Mark repeated, louder this time. "I don't have money."

"Come on. Even a buck. Every little bit helps."

"No. I don't have anything."

The man slapped the wall behind him; an echo cracked across the parking lot.

Anger nipped at Mark, blotting out all memories of the cautionary videos that had haunted his elementary school days.

"Even if I did have money, I wouldn't give it to you," he said.

The man rose, taking form. Even while limping on his good leg, he looked tall: over six feet, to be sure. Mark watched him move into the light, his features illuminated. The man's face was a craggy scar. He stared at Mark with colorless eyes.

"What did you just say to me?" the man said.

Just get him out of here. Adam's going to be here any moment.

"You don't need a taxi," Mark said. "You're lying to me."

"You think I did this to myself." Slapping his leg, grimacing. "Have some respect. You're not gonna help me out at all here?"

Mark stared into the man's face and saw pain. "No."

"Your parents didn't raise you right, did they?"

Mark's words tumbled out almost before he was even aware he'd been thinking them: "They told me never to give money to drug addicts."

The man's glare hardening, a terse advance.

"You have an addiction," Mark said. "You want money for your addiction. Admit it."

The man was intimately close now, close enough that Mark could see through his anger and into the desperation beneath.

"You don't know me," the man said. "I know guys who would bust your head for free."

The same guys who didn't show up to pick you up like they promised?

"Everybody knows guys like that," Mark said.

"Bring 'em on."

"I don't need to. I can handle myself."

They connected stares in the light. The man glanced into the store and noticed the red uniforms watching him. He didn't look angry; he looked embarrassed. Perfectly aware of his own position in relation to Mark's, and perfectly unable to shift the balance.

"Have a nice night," the man said before prowling out of the light to slip back into the shadows.

Mark watched him walking away. After a few moments, he heard the man questioning someone else. Saying his buddy left him in the middle of nowhere and he needed money for a bus, shit, actually a taxi.

Mark's body tensed when he heard Adam's voice, saying, "No, I'm sorry, I don't have anything."

Mark reacted immediately, walking across the parking lot in massive strides. He glanced at the ground, searching for bottles or other possible weapons. He found a rock, a little larger than his fist, and he picked it up. This bastard was slowing them down. Their friend might be dead and this fucker wouldn't leave them alone.

He walked to the sidewalk where the man was facing Adam. Adam, who'd toughened up a great deal after surviving childhood with his father, looked utterly unafraid of the man.

Nevertheless, Mark took action; he pushed the man from behind, forcefully enough for the guy to bend in half, as if attempting a difficult yoga pose.

"Get the fuck out of here," Mark said.

The guy whirled around, and Mark raised the rock.

"Mark, Jesus fucking Christ," Adam said. "Leave him alone. He isn't doing anything wrong."

The man nodded at Adam in appreciation before turning to Mark. "What are you gonna do with that?"

"Crack you in the temple," Mark said. "Cause permanent brain damage if you're lucky. Kill you if you're not."

"Mark, for fuck's sake, leave him alone. He just needs some help." Adam turned back to face the man. "Look, I'm sorry. If I had any money, I'd give it to you."

Mark ignored Adam and approached the man. Three feet away. Two feet.

"I'll give you ten seconds," Mark said.

Adam's skeptical eyes searched his face. Mark could sense Adam wondering if he'd really do it, and he knew that he would. He envisioned the man's skull caving, gushing blood all over the pavement.

"Nine," Mark counted down.

The man spat at his feet. "You should be ashamed, kid."

"Eight."

The man's fingers snagged a piece of Mark's shirt. Mark yanked back and swung the rock. It split the man's face just above the eyebrow, an audible crunch, and the man cried out. The impact vibrated through Mark's wrist bones.

Adam was screaming somewhere in the periphery of Mark's thoughts: "Mark. Jesus Christ what are you doing. Stop. You'll kill him."

The man crumpled and began crab-walking across the ground, blood in his eyes, dripping from his face and dotting the cement. "You fucking…" he cried. "You shit. Oh God. I just needed money for a bus." Sputtering, delirious.

Mark advanced, raising the rock over his head. The man scrambled to his feet, bony legs crisscrossing as he moved. He limp-ran away, mumbling and cursing.

Mark turned to Adam and Adam exploded. "Mark, what the fuck just happened? What's going on with you?"

"What are you talking about? He was a crazy drug addict. He might have had a knife or something."

But I don't think he did. Doesn't matter. He was slowing us down.

"You could've killed him, Mark," Adam said. "Who the fuck are you?"

"He could have killed *me*," Mark said.

"He didn't have anything to hurt you with. He was injured. Couldn't you see him limping?"

All this humanitarian bullshit from the guy who once nearly cut my arm off with a fence splinter.

"He could've been hiding a knife or something," Mark insisted.

"For Christ's sake, Mark."

"I don't back down from a fight. You know that about me."

"You call that a fight?"

"What else would I call it?"

"This was different, and you know it."

"How was it different?"

Adam shook his head in disbelief. "You know what? Fuck it. You're too far gone."

"Too far gone?"

"I don't even… Just forget it."

"What?"

"I just want to talk about finding Scott," Adam said, and he began walking toward the convenience store.

"Let's talk behind the store," Mark said. "The people inside were staring at me."

They made their way to the back of the building, avoiding each other's eyes.

Mark spoke when they were sufficiently shielded by darkness: "We're not here to talk about finding Scott. Scott is gone. We need to decide what to do now."

Adam closed his eyes for a second, registering the words. He reached into his pocket and pulled out a pack of cigarettes. He offered it to Mark. "Courtesy of my big brother," he said with a bitter smile.

Mark looked at the pack and shook his head.

Adam reached for a cigarette. Reconsidered and slipped the pack back in his pocket, returning his focus to Mark. "How do you know he's gone? Where did he go?"

"Trust me, I know. Adam, I need to tell you some important things. I need you to promise that you'll listen to me."

"After what you just did to that poor guy, I feel like I'm investing my trust in Charles fuckin' Manson right now."

"I'm serious," Mark said.

"So am I."

"Adam, for God's sake…"

"Okay, fine, I promise. Get on with it."

"I'm serious. There's no more messing around. This has gone so far out of my control."

"I'm fuckin' listening, Mark."

"Okay. The Shack. It's not just a shack."

"No fucking shit."

"I don't know what or *who* it is, but I think it wants to hurt people."

Adam laughed dryly before Mark cut him off, asking, "What?"

"This is just so ridiculous," Adam said.

"Was it ridiculous last night? Are you going to stop messing around and listen to me?"

Adam's shadow-masked face stared at him. "Why does it want to hurt people?"

"I don't know," Mark said.

"You're not giving me any fuckin' information that I didn't already have."

Mark paused before saying, "Maybe I will take a cigarette."

Adam pulled the pack out again. Mark lit his cigarette and took a deep inhale. His head fuzzed with the soft rush of nicotine.

"Okay, listen," Mark said. "I had this nightmare about the Shack a while ago. I was being chased by this, I don't know, this thing. It was the most horrible thing I've ever seen. But this is the most messed up part, Adam: the thing that was chasing me in my dream is the same thing we saw that night."

"That white light?"

"No. The thing that *made* the light."

Adam's eyes were glistening with a film of tears, his mouth a thin, tight line. "Mark, what is going on?"

"You keep asking me that. I don't know. All I know is that I'm scared. I'm scared of the Shack and I'm scared of what it can do. I feel like—"

"What?"

"I feel like we're at its mercy or something. That sounds stupid, but…"

"What do you mean?"

"I mean we have to accept that it's more powerful than us."

"Are you talking about some satanic shit or something?" Adam spat on the ground. "This is so fucked up."

"I don't know what I'm talking about, but you're absolutely right: this is fucked up. This is very fucked up. Scott is gone, and we will be questioned about it. Whatever happens, we can't say a word about the Shack. This has to be something we keep between us."

"For how long?"

"Forever. No backing out."

Adam drew a cigarette for himself and dragged on it for several seconds. He spoke through a plume of smoke: "I can't just accept that he's gone, though."

"Accept it."

Adam, narrow-eyed, assessed Mark's expression. "What's happening to you?"

"What do you mean?" Mark asked.

Adam could see something at work, something deeper than delirium and fatigue, something deeper than horror…at least, Mark suspected he could.

"You know what I mean," Adam said.

"I'm scared," Mark said, not knowing what else to say. "I've never been so scared in my life."

"I'm scared, too."

"I know."

"No, you don't know. To be honest, Mark, I'm scared of *you*."

Too far gone; that's what he said about me. Too far gone.

"I know, Adam," Mark said, keeping his voice level. "But you have to trust me on this, and you can't tell a single person about the Shack, or about what happened to Scott. This is a promise you have to make me."

"All these fuckin' promises. How many times do I need to make a promise to you?"

"Adam."

"I promise. Again."

Mark extended his hand to Adam, because this was how men sealed promises. Adam recognized the gesture, took Mark's hand and shook; the pact was bound.

"This is the last time we'll talk about this," Mark said. "If you have any questions about anything, spill them out now."

Adam stared at the ground, eyes glassy, scanning the pavement. "No." He shook his head. "There's nothing else to say."

"Good. Then it's finished. Now we just have to wait for it to blow over."

"How long will that take?"

"As long as it takes. But it *will* blow over if we play it right."

Adam nodded, eyes still cast to the ground. "Okay, I guess that's that."

Mark didn't give the words a chance to set in. "Yeah, that's that," he said. "It's late. We should probably head home." He dropped his cigarette butt, flurrying orange sparks, and crushed it under his heel.

Adam snuffed his own out presently. "You go your way, I go mine."

"That's the best plan," Mark said. "See you at school when my suspension is over."

Adam walked away, as if he hadn't even heard Mark speak. As if, perhaps, he never intended to hear him speak again. Mark didn't care, if he was to be completely honest with himself, as long as nobody else found out about the Shack.

And the moment Adam left, that was the only thing on his mind.

Chapter 12

AS HE STEPPED INSIDE HIS HOUSE, Mark saw light streaming from the kitchen. Mom called out and, for a moment, he thought that she was speaking to him.

Before he replied, though, he heard Dad shouting from upstairs: "I'm getting pretty close to dog-tired with this."

Mom, sounding sarcastic and removed, said, "I'm sorry to hear that."

"Bullshit." Dad slammed his bedroom door.

Mark paused in the doorway, hoping that maybe, just maybe, their shouting had drowned out the sound of his entrance. As he took a step toward the staircase, Mom walked out of the kitchen.

"What the hell are you doing, Mark?" she said.

Dad emerged from his bedroom and looked down. "Did you just walk in through that door?"

Mom approached Mark, grabbed him by the forearm, and looked up at Dad. "Let me talk to him."

Dad kept his eyes fixed on Mark for several paralyzing moments, then waved his hand in exasperation. "Yeah, okie-dokie, hunky-dory, all's fine, whatever." He disappeared back into his room, slamming the door again.

Mark took one look at Mom, and he could tell that she'd been crying.

"I'm sorry," he said. He was sorry for something, he just didn't know what, exactly.

"Come sit with me in the kitchen," Mom said.

Mark was relieved to hear a notable absence of anger in her voice. She sounded enervated, sad. He sat with her at the table, where she nursed a mug of English breakfast tea.

She took a few sips, slow, therapeutic. "So, are you going to tell me what's going on or do I have to ask?"

Mark was well-versed in the shaping of believable lies, in the art of the alibi.

"I went for a smoke," he said.

Mom sighed. "You don't look like you're high to me, but it's been a long time since I've smoked pot." She paused. "So I take it you were smoking cigarettes."

"Yeah, I smoked a cigarette. I don't do drugs, Mom."

"Where'd you even get it? You know what, never mind." Mom shook her head. "You shouldn't be smoking, Mark. It's bad for you."

"I know. I'm sorry."

"Why were you smoking? Did you hear us fighting?"

"No, I just wanted to smoke a cigarette."

Mom looked like she might be on the verge of smiling, but only for the briefest second. Then she leaned across the table and swatted him gently on the wrist. "You're lucky you're getting this talk from me and not from your father."

Mark remembered Dad grabbing him in the kitchen. He thought about the look that Dad got in his eyes sometimes, like he was facing a burglar instead of his own son.

"I know," he said.

Mom chuckled to herself. It was a strange and forlorn sound, and it made Mark uncomfortable.

"What?" he asked.

Mom shook her head and touched her wedding ring.

"What?" Mark repeated.

"I haven't had a cigarette in eighteen years," Mom said.

Mark smiled distantly. Mom got up to rinse her cup, then stood behind Mark and squeezed his shoulder.

"Do you have any left?" she asked.

Mark turned to face her. He could hardly believe this was his mother speaking.

"I'm sorry, Mom, I don't."

Mom huffed. "Well, it's probably for the better. I might as well shoot for nineteen years smoke-free."

They sat without speaking until, glancing at the kitchen clock, Mark realized that it was three in the morning.

"Do you mind if I go to bed?" he said. He felt a little guilty the moment he asked.

"Of course not."

Mom looked deflated as Mark rose from his chair and left the kitchen.

He slept a short and fitful sleep. Early in the morning, he heard his bedroom door open slightly.

"Mark?" Dad's voice said.

Mark kept his eyes closed. Playing dead.

"Mark, I know that Mom already spoke with you, but I'm not happy about last night, okay?"

Mark waited for his door to close, but it didn't. Dad said his name again, his voice now raised.

"Okay, Dad," he said. "It won't happen again."

"I want to see actions, *amigo*, not words. I'm off to work. See you tonight."

Mark rolled over as Dad shut the door. Sunlight beamed through his blinds, and for a few moments he experienced simple sensory bliss. Then, like remnants of a terrible dream, the previous night came back to him. He remembered Adam's terror-sick eyes, the feeling of a human skull cracking under his hand.

He wanted to go back.

Back to the Shack.

***

At half past one in the morning, Mark stood before the Shack. He forgot how suspicious Mom and Dad were getting, and he forgot the screaming that had been echoing through his mind since Scott had disappeared. He didn't know where his fear had gone, only that it had faded through some imperceptible process. Mere moments ago, that fear had been bleeding into his conscious, his unconscious, and everything in between. Like venom flooding both body and mind. Now, standing before the Shack, he was struck purely by an excitement so profound that he could barely hold himself upright.

He dropped to his knees, still facing the Shack. The dewy grass soaked through his jeans and cooled his flesh. He cast his gaze upward, like a churchgoer making an appeal to God. He admired the Shack's indescribable architecture, its seductive anonymity, its gray-black erosion. He bowed as if in prayer, forehead to the ground, breath circulating through his body in long and meditative waves. As he did this, he found himself pondering the Shack's nature: How could anything be both purely euphoric and evil at the same time? Did the Shack, in fact, *have* a nature?

He thought that he must've somehow been tricked into fearing it. If it had wanted to kill him, it would have, but it hadn't. In fact, he had no way of knowing if it had even killed Scott. All he knew was that Scott was gone.

It had been Scott's time to go, and Mark couldn't do anything about that now.

He rose back to a kneeling position. He swayed. Hoisted himself to his feet and approached the Shack as he had done so many times. As he would love to do every night for the rest of his life.

He opened the door, stepped inside.

In the darkness, without knowing why, Mark said, "I'll do whatever you say."

He felt a force, palpable, inside the Shack again. A hot and powerful current that raised all the little hairs on his body, like a surging static charge. The sensation was invigorating, even arousing. He looked toward the staircase. Although he heard no persistent thumping this time, Mark knew that he had to go up there again. He approached the stairs, coursing with the frequency of an undetectable source. He thought for a moment that the sensory input would take total control, that he would keel over sideways and faint on the spot.

He got a hold of himself, and he ascended.

The force was taking shape in his mind as a form of swirling whiteness, as a hissing sound; the Shack was speaking.

"I can hear you," Mark said.

The sound of his own voice was meek, even pathetic, in the gloom. He reached the top of the stairs and moved through the hall, his mind filled with that strange and omnipotent whiteness. He was dazed, humbled, powerless.

He reached the door to the room, the room where it had all happened—for a flicker of an instant, he heard the screams of his friends. Piercing, unharnessed, animalistic. He remembered the face inside that black fog, and he knew what it meant, and the accompanying terror came back, but only for an instant. The memory was removed by clouds of a faculty unknown; he was a servant again. He extended his hand with the precision of an archer pulling his bow, and he pushed, and the door opened.

He entered the room. Slowly, very slowly, the door closed behind him. He didn't turn at the sound, but instead stood motionless, his eyes penetrating the dark. So dark that the blackness itself became palpable, a property unto itself.

The clouds in his mind were dispersing, and words leaked through the mist, disconnected but not unintelligible. The words in his own voice said *stay* and *go* with equal urgency, but there were also words in another voice…words he could hear distantly, but that he could not yet quite make out.

A beacon of light materialized before him, a glaring and centralized shaft. A silhouette moved from the back of the room and into the light. It was the nightmare shape. Its pallid flesh rose with breath beneath the tatters of its clothing. Its bones shifted like pistons as it glided with disturbing grace. It looked at Mark with its shifting, inaccessible idea of a face, the impression of eyes where eyes should be.

Despite the energy fogging his mind, Mark heard a whisper of horror screaming in his unconscious. His eyes dewed with tears.

His sense of unease was just as quickly muffled, immobilized, and then killed. "What do you want?" he asked. He was again taken aback by the smallness of his own voice. He braced himself for a response.

Like some perverse monument, the nightmare shape stood in the light without the slightest trace of motion.

"Please tell me," Mark said. "Please."

The head, if it could be called a head, tilted upward, exposing the underside of an inhuman chin. Something like a laugh, rattling and airy, filled the Shack. The mouth and jaw, sealed with vague resemblances of flesh and tissue, flickered with the illusion of motion while also maintaining the appearance of motionlessness. Mark wondered if the laugh might've come from his own mouth.

A wavering smile made its way to his face. The nightmare shape's head slanted forward, unfeeling sockets imploring Mark's face.

"You…" Mark said, unthinkingly.

The thing nodded. Its arm, thin as naked bone, extended.

"…I…"

The arm quivered, twitched, the impression of orgasmic response. Fingers flicking the air.

"We."

The verbal sequence had an uncanny impact on Mark, a removal of anxious thought. Words that emerged, unscathed, through his brain-mist; a pact, a doctrine. Hieroglyphics in fog. He couldn't pinpoint or locate any association with the words, but he still sensed them, registered their affect.

"You. I. We."

There was an essence to this utterance, to these three words, to this vocal inscription: You. I. We.

Mark's mind was momentarily awash in aural flashbacks: the thumping in his closet, the wild, frenzied cries of Scott and Adam.

"What do you want me to do?" he asked.

The nightmare shape was back to a static position, arms hanging at its sides, its sockets communicating sense through blackness.

"I'm ready now," Mark said. "I can hear you."

The mist distilled his consciousness and he did not resist. The nightmare shape's voice began to register, despite the smoky supernatural coating that swirled like sleeping gas in Mark's brain.

Kill, the voice said.

"Kill who?" Mark said. He looked at the deathly face with doubt. "I can't kill anyone."

Not just you: you/I/we.

"It's not only that I won't, or that I don't want to. Look at the size of me. I'm a kid."

Kill. The weight of the command pierced through the fog.

Mark stared down, unnerved by the nightmare face and its sickly, amorphous features.

He studied the nightmare shape, and it pointed behind him, to the corner of the room. He turned his attention to the corner, and he watched physical objects materialize, strands and particles pulling into shape. He couldn't yet distinguish what was appearing, but he watched intently. The word *kill* reverberated in his mind.

He saw himself appear; not only was it his own body, but his own clothing as well. The same clothing that he was wearing at this very moment. His double was awash in dim white light, stooping to the floor to pick something up.

The motion was familiar. Mark was observing a moment from last night, when he'd found the rock in the parking lot. A hybrid of recording and performance.

It couldn't be real.

Mark began to approach his double, but the nightmare shape held a hand toward him. *Stop and watch*, the gesture said.

And so he watched and, as he watched, his every belief about reality began to slip away. It chilled him to feel how smoothly, how effortlessly, the solid foundation of what *could* happen liquefied into a confrontation with what *was* happening. He was watching a living, moving version of himself, replaying moments from the past. Insanity, like fear, reached through the fog and clawed his thoughts.

Double Mark advanced on the man who had asked for money. Double Man didn't even see it coming. The impact of the rock was solid, vicious, visceral.

Mark heard cracking bone. He saw the spurt of blood.

Then, like a sports highlight instant replay, he watched the moment again; he watched his arm move with brutal intent. He watched the rock connect. Heard the sounds. Saw the blood.

Watched it again.

Saw the blood. Heard the crack. Saw the blood.

The crack of rock splitting bone, a skull fractured in the space of a syllable. Mark didn't know how many times he was forced to watch and hear the assault, but it began to acquire new meaning; it became fluid, hypnotic, natural.

Then, as quickly as it had appeared, the scene vanished.

Kill.

Chapter 13

THE NEXT MORNING, MARK AWOKE TO the sound of voices.

Emerging from a dreamless half-sleep, he listened. The voices weren't familiar. They were the curt, artificial voices of law officials: "We only need a moment of his time." "We just have a few questions, and then we'll be out of your way." "If you wouldn't mind, ma'am, thank you, ma'am."

Mark heard his mother climbing the stairs. He got out of bed, pulled on some clothes, and tried to fix his hair.

Mom rapped her knuckles on his door.

"Come in," he said.

The door opened a crack and Mom's face, concerned, peered through the opening. Her eyes flicked across his face for what seemed like half a minute.

"Yes?" Mark said, trying to sound calm.

"There are two police officers here," Mom said. "They want to speak with you." She sounded like she was reading from a script, or citing a passage from a crime novel.

"About what?" Mark asked.

"About Scott. He still hasn't turned up."

Mark heard distant accusation in her voice. He attempted to look shocked as he said, "Okay, give me a minute."

The door closed and he sat on the bed, struggling for air. He struggled to control his breathing, eyes closed, fingers laced on his lap. Thinking that the cops might get restless, he rose, released a quaking stream of air, and walked out of his room.

There were two of them standing in the doorway: crew cuts, faces that looked aged somewhere between the early thirties and mid-forties, muscular builds, unfeeling expressions, uniforms, handcuffs, guns. Matching archetypes of authority.

"Thank you again, ma'am," the officer on the left said. "We'll try to scoot off and get out of your way as soon as we can."

They removed their boots and entered the kitchen.

Mark walked in after them. "Hi," he said.

They turned.

"Mark?" The one on the right spoke this time.

"Yeah."

The one who had spoken nodded. "I'm Officer Thompson." He smiled a policeman smile. "This is Officer Selby. How are you doing this morning?"

"Okay," Mark said. "Tired."

Thompson laughed a short, braying laugh and Selby fixed bulldog eyes, all pupil and no bullshit, on Mark.

"Well, let's make sure you can get back to bed soon, then," Thompson said. "When I was your age I was practically—what do they call it—you know, like a hamster—"

"Diurnal?" Selby offered, but even he didn't look convinced that it was the word Thompson was looking for.

"Nocturnal, that's what it was," Thompson said, quaking with another terse guffaw.

Mark and the officers stood in the center of the kitchen, semicircle.

Mom spoke up. "Please, feel free to take a seat at the table."

"Thank you, ma'am," Thompson said.

The officers lowered themselves into undersized kitchen chairs, emitting synchronized *ohhhh*s as they did so.

Mark sat across from them, focusing all his energy on the maintenance of a neutral expression. He'd been through many interrogations in the principal's office; he'd practised and solidified techniques of bluffing and understatement. But this situation was different, existing as it did beyond his school's fairy-tale construct and all its accompanying niceties and regulations.

"Okay, Mark," Thompson said. "We're here because, as you know, your friend Scott went missing a few nights ago."

Mark nodded what he thought to be a good, convincing nod: a proper balance of affirmation and restraint. Selby stared, canine, in return and asked Mark where Scott had been that night. Mark said he didn't know.

"When is the last time you saw him, if you were to, you know, make a guess?" Thompson asked.

"I don't remember exactly."

"Remember," Selby said.

Mark met Selby's gaze and, studying his guard-dog eyes, he saw only instinct and aggression.

"I can't remember." Mark diverted his focus from Selby to Thompson. The roles of good cop and bad cop, as designated by every television program, film, or novel that dealt with crime, had been clearly assigned to these two men. Mark recognized the roles, and he knew where to invest his hesitant loyalty.

"Did you see him the day he went missing?" Thompson asked.

"No," Mark said. "It was definitely before that."

"How do you know?" Selby asked.

Adrenaline, like an intravenous rush, drowned Mark's sense. He'd fucked up already. The cops hadn't specified when Scott had disappeared. He would need to slow down. He might need to act out his fatigue to the brink of excess, use it as an excuse for slower response time.

His mind wandered in another direction, imagining Selby in the Shack: Selby's eyes darting in terror, beefy arms reaching, helpless, toward that unstoppable white light. Mark imagined himself advancing, rock in hand. He imagined his skinny arm thrusting and pumping, deadly precision, and the heavy whacking sound of stone punching through muscle. He imagined Selby whimpering like a puppy, writhing and twitching, gripping gashes on his body, gouts of gore bursting from his face and stomach. Currents of blood pumping from his ears.

Mark's fantasy eased his fear, and he found the will to speak: "Well, my mom told me the very next day that he had gone missing. I didn't leave my house the day before he disappeared."

"Why not?" Selby asked. "It was a weekday. Didn't you go to school?"

Mark tried to decode the question, to uncover its second meaning, if it had any. He deduced that Selby, that fucker, probably knew that Mark had been suspended. Selby was trying to humiliate him.

"No, I didn't," Mark said. "I was suspended from school this week."

The flesh along Selby's jaw pulsed, barely containing the massive bone beneath. "Why were you suspended, Mark?"

"I got into a fight."

"Wasn't the first time, was it?" Selby said.

"No."

Selby gave Thompson a knowing look, which Thompson appeared to ignore, instead staring at Mark with a legal amount of sentiment.

"I'm sure you're upset that your friend has gone missing, Mark," Thompson said.

"Yeah. Yeah, I am."

Thompson studied Mark's face, then gave a curt nod. "All right, sorry to bother you folks. Officer Selby and I will leave you with our personal information. If anything comes up, anything at all, that you think might help us find Scott, please give us a call."

Selby remained seated, staring at Mark, as Thompson stood. Mark alternately stared into space and met Selby's gaze with confusion, timing his shifts in focus with as much discretion as he could summon.

"Okay, I think that's everything." Thompson wiped his hands, as if they were covered with invisible chalk dust. He looked down at Selby. "You ready to go?"

"Yeah," Selby said. "Yeah, I'm ready to go." He maintained his stare on Mark, level and militant, even as he stood.

Mark remained at the table as Mom accompanied the cops to the door. They placated her with more police niceties: "Thanks again for your time, ma'am." "Let us know if you need anything." "We hope he'll turn up soon."

The door closed, and Mom returned to the kitchen.

"Are you okay, Mark?" she asked.

"Yeah, I'm just worried about Scott."

"I know." She still didn't sound convinced.

***

Mark was uneasy on Monday morning. As he made his way to the bus stop, he came to expect the squealing of a cop car at the curb. He thought of Selby's flat eyes peering through the crack of a half-unrolled window, and he thought of that low, law official voice saying, "All right, kid, get in. Game over." His agitation increased when he arrived at school, when he couldn't help but recall that Scott and Adam normally met him at the same spot every morning. Today he walked alone and in silence, trying to avoid the nagging eyes of his peers. The stories must have spread by now: stories about his fight with Clinton, stories about Scott's disappearance. And, in the true spirit of second-hand or third-hand or thirtieth-hand stories, the retellings would inevitably be divorced from anything that resembled reality.

Mark heard Madeline's voice as he neared the school tarmac, calling his name. In that instant, he came slowly back to himself, to the conditions of the present. He stopped and waited for her.

"So, you're back," she said. "You did your time."

"Yeah," Mark said.

Her Madeline smile: it didn't take Mark long to realize how much he'd missed that smile, even if it had only been missing from the madness of his life for a week.

"I don't think Clinton wants to fight you again," Madeline said.

"I don't want to fight again, either."

"Really?"

Mark shrugged. "Of course not. I never wanted to fight him in the first place."

"What's with the tone there, man?" Madeline said.

Mark, still finding his footing in this particular pocket of reality, realized how hostile he might've sounded, and he looked down at his shoes.

How does she do this to me? How can she make me feel so goddamn aware of myself?

"Sorry, I didn't mean to get annoyed with you," he said.

"I assume you sounded that way because you don't want me to get the wrong impression, and not because you're a grouchy asshole," she said. "Right?"

"Right."

As the gap in their conversation extended, Mark began to feel desperate. He didn't want her to leave. If nothing else, he wanted an excuse to see her smile again, but he could not seem to find a new topic of conversation, no matter how hard he tried.

His world seemed more and more like a widening fissure. No matter how fleetingly, Madeline allowed him to see something else, something on the threshold.

Say something. Say something.

"I heard about Scott," Madeline said, alleviating his self-pressure only to replace it with new tension. "That he went missing. He still hasn't turned up, has he?"

"No, he's still missing."

"That's terrible. Seriously. I mean, you guys seem like you're really good friends. I always see you with each other in the halls and everything."

A cold lump settled in Mark's throat. "Yeah. He's my best friend. He and Adam."

"Adam looked really upset about it," Madeline said. "I don't really talk to him or anything, but I could tell, just by looking at him. You know?"

"Yeah."

Madeline's stare took hold of Mark, and his internal voice screamed at him to say something beyond the monosyllabic, to say the right words.

"Thanks for talking to me," he mustered.

Madeline's look began to soften. "I just…" Her bangs fell in her eyes and she shook them away, turning her head. "…I don't know, I care, I guess."

"Well, thank you for caring."

She set her eyes on his face again. "Can I tell you something?"

"Yeah."

"I think I like you. The hell if I know why. You're pretty damn strange and we haven't really talked much, but… I don't know… You're—"

"What?"

"I don't know. I really don't."

"You don't know."

"No, I don't know."

"I'm what?"

"I don't know. Yeah, you're strange, but that's not it."

"Strange."

"What, you don't like that word? Okay, let me use a nice, pretty word. You're *unique*." She rolled her eyes and laughed. "Is that better? How's that sound?"

"Unique?"

"Yeah, unique. Fuck, I don't know what word to use. Maybe there isn't a word. I don't think you're downright weird or anything—at least, I hope you aren't. Look, stop fishing, it's the best I can come up with."

Mark, uncomfortable, broke into a half-smile. She reciprocated, and all his defenses fell to the wayside.

"I don't think many people would agree with you," Mark said. "I think most people do find me weird."

"Why do you get that feeling?"

Mark, considering the question, realized he didn't have an immediate answer. He barely spoke to anyone at school aside from Adam and Scott, so how could he know what anyone thought of him? Maybe it was the subtle avoidance he noticed from his peers, the way people redirected their eyes when he looked at them.

"I don't know. Maybe I'm nuts," he said.

Madeline laughed a strained laugh. "You should come over sometime."

The invitation was abrupt, unexpected. Mark's nervousness peaked. He ran his fingertips through his hair, cleared his throat, scratched the back of his neck and shifted on the spot.

"I mean, if you want to," Madeline said.

"I do," Mark said. "I really do."

"Well, then… How about after school today?"

Mark's excitement relented to a pang of guilt. He had always wanted this, on some level, to spend time with Madeline, alone…but he had to be available for the Shack. He missed it.

Needed it.

The conflict formed a tumult of screaming impulses in his brain, all of them vying urgently for his attention. Nothing and nobody had the kind of instant, startling impact on him that Madeline had. She brought him to himself. Within minutes, the nightmare of his situation had come to a standstill. He couldn't ignore the way that Madeline, only Madeline, spoke to him any more easily than he could ignore the intensity of her stare, or the sense of calm that accompanied her smile. He could not ignore Madeline.

But the Shack… His inner voice crept in, and he stifled it. "Yeah, sure, today works," he finally replied.

"Okay, good."

The bell rang, and as it did, it struck Mark that this was the longest conversation he had ever had with Madeline Fraley.

"Well, I have to head to class," he said.

"I might just join you."

"Oh yeah, that's right. You're in my math class."

Get it together. The voices in his head were still screaming, and still no voice rose above any other.

Chapter 14

WHEN SCHOOL WAS OUT FOR THE day, Mark waited outside the front exit and watched the flood of students spilling across the tarmac in a hubbub of conversation and laughter.

As the crowd thinned, Adam walked out, staring ahead with sunken eyes.

Selfishly, irrationally, Mark hoped that Adam wouldn't see him. He remained silent and motionless.

Where's Madeline?

Adam turned his head, stopped, and surveyed Mark. He circumvented verbal exchange, articulating through mannerisms instead; he stooped over and groaned, like a drunk about to vomit.

"Adam, you okay?" Mark said. He was possessed by the disquieting thought that somebody, anybody, might be watching them right now, and the extended thought that somebody, anybody, might get suspicious.

"No, I'm fucking not okay," Adam said.

"Stand up," Mark said. "If anybody looks at you right now, they're going to think something's wrong."

Adam gathered himself and walked toward Mark. "For fuck's sake, Mark. Something *is* wrong."

Mark saw a bruise painting the side of Adam's face purple; he pointed at the swollen mark, grimacing. "What happened?"

"The fuckin' cops showed up at my house, asking all these questions about Scott. My dad just watched them talking to me, drinkin' and drinkin' the whole time. Hey, officers, he said, would you like a drink, like it was no big deal, but he was getting shitfaced in front of them. After they left, I tried to walk down to my room, but he grabbed my arm and said he knew something was up. I tried to walk away, but he wouldn't let me go. Mark, he fucking went off on me. You've seen my dad lose it." He paused, and Mark nodded. "This was one of the worst times. He tried to beat the information out of me. He took a can opener to my stomach, man, and started rolling it along, fuckin' pulling me apart. I just kept saying I had no idea where Scott was. Thank God he was so drunk, I was able to fight him off. Otherwise he might have fucking killed me. The whole time he was doing it, he had this look like he was someplace else. Zoned out, you know? And he kept saying, really quietly, you know, that he just wanted to get to the bottom of all this. While pinching my skin in that opener and twisting and twisting. Oh Jesus…"

Mark reflected on Adam's dad, his methodical and deliberate nature. His brutality wasn't comprised of merely spontaneous eruptions. No, Adam's dad could find *any* means to cause pain, and his selections were often insidiously elaborate. Like, for instance, when he'd locked Adam inside the garage in the winter; or the morning he'd pinned Adam's arm against the side of his van and slammed the door against Adam's wiggling fingers. Adam had been eight years old at the time.

It wasn't just that Adam's dad was *mean*; he was strategic.

At this moment, Mark had to consider his own safety. Adam, like anyone else, was capable of folding under pressure. Especially the kind of pressure that came along with Adam's dad under the influence of too much liquor.

"Did you tell him anything?" Mark asked.

"Of course I fuckin' didn't. What would I say? *Okay, Dad, you win. Here's what went down: Scott got swallowed up by a haunted house.* Right? The truth would've hurt me more than saying nothing."

"It's not a haunted house," Mark said.

Adam stared at him, disbelieving, and snorted. "You've lost it. No doubt about it. Don't talk to me."

"I won't," Mark said, "but don't forget that you were involved in this thing as much as I was."

Adam's face, contorted, drew closer to Mark's. "You were the one who dragged us there. Don't forget it, you fucking psychopath."

Mark swallowed. "I don't remember you refusing to join me. I remember both of you voluntarily coming with me to the Shack that night. Don't try to pin this on me. If you don't want to talk to me, that's fine, but you are every bit as much to blame as me."

"Go to hell, Mark. Burn in hell with your fucking Shack. I should've set the thing on fire when I had the chance. Fuck knows I thought about it so many times."

Mark lunged, unthinking, a clumsy swipe for the front of Adam's shirt.

Backing away, Adam said, "Stay the hell away from me. You're sick. You're losing your fuckin' mind."

Mark didn't move. His breath, hot, coursed up his throat like something poisonous. His thoughts were suddenly awash in the repellent image of his own reflection: a face that was lacking something crucial. *Am I losing my mind? Is it already lost?*

In that instant, Madeline walked out. She stopped and shot her eyes between Mark and Adam, unease written all over her face.

"Mark, what are you doing?" she asked.

She sounded as if she'd found him holding Adam at gunpoint which, figuratively speaking, Mark supposed she had. Mark and Adam exchanged a look, unmistakably bitter, then drew further away from each other.

"Nothing," Mark replied. "Are you ready to go?"

"Are you guys okay?" Madeline asked.

Adam was already walking away.

"Everything's fine," Mark said. "We had an argument. We always have arguments. You know how it is." He followed Adam's retreating back with his eyes before turning to Madeline and smiling a strained smile.

She didn't reciprocate.

"You two sounded really angry. It didn't just sound like a little argument. Maybe you should go talk to him," she said.

"No, I think it'll be better if I just leave it."

"What were you arguing about?"

"I don't know. Nothing, really. I think he's just upset because his dad's an asshole."

"That's too bad that he would take it out on you."

"It happens. I'm over it already." Mark knew that his excuse wasn't very believable. To avoid letting it set in, he changed the topic. "Are we going to your house?"

If the conversation had gone any further, he might've found himself disclosing the truth (at least in part), and that was something to avoid. The last thing he wanted to do was discuss the Shack with Madeline, not only because it was too important to him, but because Madeline was too important.

***

Madeline lived in an old neighborhood close to the school, a neighborhood that in no way resembled the pastel-faced wonderland in which Mark had been raised. This area was full of seasoned duplexes and weather-faded rental properties.

Stepping into Madeline's house, Mark smelled stale cigarette smoke and old books. He looked at Madeline while unlacing his shoes and, as always, her beauty made him absurdly nervous.

"Are your parents home?" he asked.

She shrugged, a gesture accompanied with a knowing look. Mark's insides buzzed and he enjoyed the sensation.

"Do you want to watch TV or something?" Madeline asked.

Mark tried to keep his eyes on her, tried not to lose his mask of normalcy.

"Yeah, okay," he said.

They walked into the living room and the smoky smell intensified. Everything in the room showed its age. Mark sat on a faded couch that probably used to be maroon, but was now an unnameable shade of brown. He scanned the multi-cracked spines of books aligning a shelf: bestsellers and genre fiction, mostly. Madeline sat close beside him, close enough that her thigh pressed against his. His heart felt like it might just pump itself out of his chest cavity, leap up through his throat and land, twitching and spurting, on her unvacuumed carpet.

"Is there anything you want to watch?" she asked. "We could always just talk."

"Yeah, that would be fine, too."

She gave him a Madeline smile.

"I like your house," he said.

"Thanks," she said. "It's cool, I guess."

"I like it."

Madeline laughed and rolled her eyes. She touched his arm, a whisper of fingertips. He looked down at her hand, then up at her eyes, fervent, full of colour. He forced a cough.

"What's your house like?" she asked.

Her hand still there. Not only touching, but holding. Physical affect, sustained.

Mark strained to keep his voice flat and level. "Not like this. My house looks like everybody else's house. It's nice. My parents keep it clean. I don't know. It's a house."

Mark's thoughts, boundless, roamed from the warmth and shape of Madeline's leg to the blank exterior of his kitchen, submitting finally to the Shack.

Madeline's voice, rupturing his distance, spoke his name.

"Yeah?" he said. "Sorry."

"It's okay. You seem, I don't know…zoned out or, I don't know. Something. What are you thinking about?"

"Sorry. I'm just thinking about my house, I guess."

Madeline laughed. "You don't make it sound like there's a lot to think of it, man."

Mark laughed too. "Yeah, I guess not."

"Do you get along well with your parents?" Madeline asked.

Mark thought this might be the first time he'd ever been asked such a question outside the principal's office. In the presence of Weatherill, he was guarded by the motions of a guise. With Madeline, he felt as if he had actually heard the question, and he actually wanted to answer it.

"I don't think I know them very well," he said.

"Ha."

"That sounds weird, doesn't it?"

"Kind of, yeah."

"They're parents," Mark said. "They feed me. They do things like that. You know, they say, *Do your homework*. That's really it. It's difficult to explain."

Madeline leaned toward him; the gentle slope of her neck, her tied hair undoing, loose hairs tickling the skin there.

He pulled away, no rationality, his brain screaming, *You are an idiot, You are a fuckup*.

"What about you?" Mark asked.

"What, am I too fast?" A whispering, her hand still there.

His body in torment. "No."

She pulled back nevertheless, gave a half-smile. "My parents are divorced, so I don't see my dad much, but he's just a shitty guy. He was cheating on my mom for a long time. Found a woman online and I think he's still with her. He did the usual cheating parent thing, you know… He would lie to my mom to cover up all his nights away from home. He created this, like, elaborate world. Said his estranged brother had turned up, and that they were meeting up regularly to set things straight. They were the weirdest, most detailed things, these stories he would come up with. I think, on some level, he actually thought his own fictional set-up was true. My mom's pretty cool, though. She lets me do what I want. I smoked up with her once."

Mark was amused by the image of Dad passing him a joint with one hand, eating a forkful of wet green vegetables with the other. He chuckled.

"What?" Madeline said, a note of self-defence inflecting her voice.

"Nothing. I was just thinking about how weird it would be to smoke weed with my parents."

"Oh." Madeline laughed with him. "That's what my friends usually say. I guess it's kind of unusual."

The dreaded pause, Mark unable to respond.

"Thanks for asking me to come over," he said eventually. "I always wanted to talk to you more often than I do."

A moment after he spoke, his excitement mutated into pure anxiety, a knot in the bottom of his stomach.

"I always wanted to talk to you, too, but I didn't know what to say," she said.

"Why not?"

"I don't know, why did *you* never talk to *me*?"

"I don't know. You're really pretty."

Madeline didn't react to the compliment, staring into space instead. "You always seemed… How can I phrase this without insulting you?"

Mark tried to look reassuringly at her, but he probably looked like he had gas pain instead. "You won't insult me."

"You always look kind of angry, to be honest. I know you've been in a lot of fights, but it's not that. It's the way you look sometimes."

Mark tried to imagine how he might appear to an observer, but he couldn't bring himself to do it; instead, he again pictured his own reflection. Reflection on reflection, haunting. He gave a slow nod before allowing his eyes to drift down, where he felt most comfortable to look.

"Don't get me wrong, though," Madeline said. "You don't seem angry right now."

The obligatory pause.

"I like you," she added.

For one mad moment, Mark was tempted to tell her that there were scary things happening to him. So many scary things.

Instead he offered the commonplace response: "I like you too, Madeline."

She leaned in again, tilted his face, and pressed her lips against his. His eyes still open, surprised, seeing her eyes closed. Eyelashes long enough to touch her cheeks. He could smell her: perfume, shampoo, scents he liked immediately. He was excited by the closeness, the damp warmth of her mouth against his. Flesh to flesh. He realized that he wasn't even kissing her back, that he was, in fact, reclined stiffly on the couch. Rigor mortis. She pulled away, looking at him for a few seconds, covering her mouth.

"That was my first kiss," Mark said abruptly. "I'm sure I could be better."

She rested her hand on his knee, and her touch dissuaded his tension a little.

"It was fine, Mark. I guess I'm nervous, too," she said.

"That's good, then."

She shook her head, playful, a look of disbelief. He was messing this up. What was the matter with him? He was saying the wrong things, doing the wrong things.

"I don't know why I'm nervous, though," Madeline said. "I mean, I've kissed a lot of people. You're just… I don't know, you're Mark…"

Mark stood up, sweat pasting his palms to his jeans; he glanced at Madeline, frantic, apologetic, and he left the room.

"What are you doing?" Madeline asked. "Hey, Mark, relax. Everything's cool."

Her voice sounded concerned, like she could see inside him. Like she could see the Shack. He squeezed his eyes shut, grabbed at his hair, walked toward her door.

"Mark, what's going on?" Madeline touched, then pulled, at the back of his shirt.

Her protest was empathetic, not threatening, but Mark was in a panic. He made his way outside and he ran down the street, ghastly voices cascading through his mind, assailing his senses, guiding him to the only place where he knew he belonged.

Fear was an afterthought as soon as he turned the corner.

Chapter 15

MARK SAT ON THE SHACK'S GRAY floor, cross-legged. Closed his eyes. Audible atmosphere. A frequency, so intimate, that left imprints on his body in the most secret of places. He drew the fibrous, musty smell of aged bark into his nostrils. Some instinctive corner of his psyche anticipated the return of the rhythmic thump, the re-emergence of that nightmare shape in material form.

Instead, the Shack was as superficially nonresponsive as it had been upon his first visit. He relished the solitude for an hour or two before forcing himself to rise. The cliché, *all good things end eventually*, needled his brain. He ignored it.

He spent one more minute in the Shack and stepped out into the waning daylight.

When he got home, he saw a squad car parked in the driveway. For a moment, he considered turning around, walking away. As quickly as the Shack had calmed him, his peace was stolen by the sight of that car. He had the crazed but very momentary urge to run back to Madeline's house, to knock on her door. To give himself another chance. The temptation disintegrated as Officer Selby stepped out.

"Mark," Selby said. "Come here."

Mark eyed the man with caution as he approached him. He stopped about a meter away, electing to remain silent. Selby beckoned him with a thick index finger. Mark took a single step, stopping again.

"Where were you after school?" Selby asked.

"Why?"

Selby made a sound. "Don't be smart."

"I was at a girl's house," Mark said.

"A girl, huh?" Selby raised his eyebrows, patronizing. "You got a girlfriend, Mark?"

"She's not my girlfriend."

Selby sucked his lower lip, a tense hissing sound. "Look, I don't have anything to ask you, okay? I have something to tell you." He bent at the waist, pressed his big hands against his thighs, and, with an unflinching glare, he pinned Mark where he stood. "I've seen your school records. I've been asking the other kids about you, and there's something you should know. I know you're not innocent. You can keep pulling this cute bullshit all you want, but I know you had something to do with Scott's disappearance. Let's get that clear now."

Mark's heart jack-hammered, but he maintained his expressionless stare. "How can you know something that isn't true?" he said.

Selby ran his fingers over his own stubbled head and said, "You'll be seeing me again soon." He got into his car and sped out of the cul-de-sac.

As Mark watched the car depart, he wished he could will his own heart into beating at a normal pace. When he entered his house, he saw his parents waiting in the living room, wearing frowns that matched.

"Hi, Mom. Hi, Dad," he said.

A useless attempt to sustain the illusion. Mom and Dad looked at each other, then Mom gave Dad a subtle nod and Dad nodded back. They both turned toward their son.

"What was that police officer just talking with you about?" Dad asked.

Be cool. Just take it easy and everything will be fine.

"Just now?" Mark said, buying time.

Dad stared at him coldly. During the short-lived delay, Mark's mind ran through a catalogue of half-invented responses.

"Yes, just now," Dad said. "On the driveway."

"He doesn't trust me," Mark said. "I don't know why." He took a step back, toward the staircase.

"I know why he doesn't trust you, Mark. I think this is an important lesson for you to learn," Dad said. His voice quavered, a hazy veneer disguising anger.

"I do, too," Mom said.

"What lesson?" Mark said. "I didn't do anything." He retreated another step.

"It doesn't matter whether or not you did anything. Have you ever heard of the age-old expression, *guilty by association*?" Dad asked.

"No." Mark was lying. He'd heard the expression, of course, but it was best to give Dad the space to sermonize, to speak his words and make his impact the way he wanted to make it.

"It means once somebody has gotten into enough trouble, they're going to get blamed for all kinds of things, even if they didn't do anything," Dad said. Rage now punctuated his speech.

"That isn't fair. That isn't the way it should be," Mark said. He stood still, gauging the situation.

"It doesn't matter whether or not it's fair, Mark. It's the way the cookie cooks," Dad said.

"So what do you want me to do?"

Mom and Dad exchanged a long look, Dad shaking his head in aggravation before bolting up, suddenly, and grabbing Mark by the forearm. Not hard enough to hurt, but hard enough to keep him in place.

"I want you to be normal, for Christ's sake," Dad said.

"Honey, stop that," Mom said.

Dad released his grip, and Mark took the opportunity to bolt up the stairs. He was careful not to shut the door with too much force. The last thing he needed was to suffer through a lecture about slamming doors. He pressed his back against the wall, slid to a sitting position.

He revisited his Selby-occupied fantasy: Selby's dumbfounded face, streaming with droplets of his own cerebral blood.

Suddenly, a rupturing thump.

The sound in the closet was back. Mark's heart bobbed in the bottom of his throat. He stood, ignoring an insurmountable sense of terror, ignoring everything. He advanced toward the closet door. He got close enough to feel the reverberation of the sound. Close enough to sense a presence behind. He closed his fingers around the handle. Pulled.

The instant he opened the door, fear took charge of his mind.

A long, blood-streaked shape gripped the carpet between his feet and tugged itself forward. For one brief, sickening moment, he thought the shape was a severed arm. Perhaps a severed arm would've been more tolerable than the thing in front of him. At least he would be able to recognize the shape and actuality of a human arm. This thing couldn't be real. It couldn't exist.

He was unable to look away, horror as paralysis, a desperate effort to process that this thing was physical and wet and slithering across his bedroom carpet.

Although it was the length of a human arm, he now realized that it was much thicker. It had the heavy, bulging width of a python, and the texture of something alien, something seen only on television screens or in vividly bad dreams. Its skin was translucent, gray-white, like some kind of strange larva. The imprints of organs pumped and glistened beneath its flesh. Its face was conical, predatory, bristling with mandibles. A cluster of tarantula-like eyes stared inhumanly upward, glinting dully in the light. A bundle of slimy, exoskeletal tendrils slipped from its mouth, tugged at the carpet, and pulled the body forward.

Mark wanted so badly to cry out. He backed away. The tendrils ripped a clump of carpet free and the thing lurched forward with the same distinct thump that had been haunting Mark's sleep.

Mark fell backward. His head connected with the corner of his bedside table. He grunted in pain, his eyes still fixed on the creature's approach.

It moved with impossible speed, tendrils clutching like fingers, yanking the serpentine body. When it was mere feet away from Mark, it hoisted itself up, the lower end supporting the hideous, ichor-spattered upper half. The heavy head bobbed in the air, countless eyes staring, the intent to kill inscribed on those damp insect globes.

Although his entire body was rattling with fear, Mark managed to reach behind himself and grab the legs of his bedside table. The thing dropped down to a slithering position again, tendrils digging into the carpet like roots, pulling with impossible strength.

Mark yanked blindly at the small table, animalistic fright, his eyes focused on the creature. His index finger slid across a loose nail protruding from the wood; his skin sheared open, a horrible sting. He drew his fingers away, stared at his hand through a daze of fear and pain. Blood ran from his fingertip in a thick scarlet stream, dotting the carpet with heavy beads.

The thing rose again and emitted an awful hissing sound. The sound of something ready to feed. Mark exclaimed and, despite his pain, lifted the bedside table over his head. The lamp slid off and tumbled to the floor, bumping and thudding against the wall.

Don't let Mom and Dad hear.

He brandished the table like some oversized weapon, hyperventilating, waiting for the thing to come close enough.

It drew forward another two feet. Warm, moist air gusted from its tendril-clogged mouth. The odor was vicious, like meat gone putridly off. Without thinking, Mark brought the table over his head and slammed it down. It struck with surprising force, the edge diving through the creature's body and crunching against the floor beneath.

The creature released a squealing, rattling cry. Its tendrils lashed and whipped, spraying blackish saliva and blood.

Its bottom half pulled free with a squelching rip. The top half continued tugging, beady eyes channeling hunger and hatred.

Can it hate?

Wordlessly, soundlessly, Mark swung again. He split the creature's head lengthwise, cleaving its cluster of eyes with a single motion. A black fountain of fluid spurted from the wound. It rained on Mark's arms in hot streams, like thick soup sputtering from a boiling-over pot.

The creature continued screaming for a few seconds, then froze and went silent.

Mark had killed it.

He yanked the gore-painted table away, numb from panic and fear. He took a moment to register the scene: the mangled body of an otherworldly creature leaking lifeblood all over his carpet, his arm slick with its eye juice and a drying line of his own blood. He was lightheaded and dazed. He set the table back in its place; it was flecked with bits of hard gray flesh, sprinkled with colorless blood. He became strangely entranced by the sight of the viscera, tangible and dangerous and real.

Eventually he shifted his gaze to the creature again, and the image before him caused him to scream. It was not a monstrous, arachnid-faced thing he saw on his bedroom carpet.

It was the twitching body of his friend, Scott.

He immediately recognized the once-timid face, now contorted in a grimace of obscene agony. There was a wide gash between the eyes, and cuts on the torso, gurgling and red. The neatly pressed shirt, family-function-conservative, was tattered and bloodied. And he, Mark, had landed the blows that had made those marks.

Scott's body lurched and Mark yelled again, rigid with horror.

Mark felt the nightmare shape as an invasion of his thoughts, turning his arms into gooseflesh. Somewhere in the distance, his parents were calling him, asking if everything was okay. Voices growing frantic.

Scott was lying on his floor, pummelled to death.

Mark pressed his sweat-slicked palms against his eyes, hard enough to feel the sockets beneath. He continued pushing, redness washing his vision. After some time, he mustered the courage to peel his hands away. He opened his eyes, and the pressure he'd applied began to disappear slowly, starry beads speckling his sight.

Looking down again, he saw that the body was not in fact Scott's. Again, he was looking at the shrivelled body of the creature he'd just killed.

What. The. Fuck.

Dad knocked on the door, asking why he was screaming.

Panic took precedence over everything. He managed to form a response: "Sorry, I dozed off and had a bad dream."

Weak, unconvincing. His reply was met with a long, skeptical pause on the other side of the door.

"A bad dream," Dad repeated.

"Yes," Mark said. "A nightmare."

"A nightmare."

"A bad nightmare," Mark said.

Another pause. "Mark, I'd like to come in."

"Just give me a minute, Dad." He was trying to suppress the fear in his voice, and he knew he was failing.

What if his father was to walk in right at this moment, stand beside him, and stare down at the mangled corpse of this snakelike thing? He imagined Dad asking, *What've you been up to in here?* The absurd thought looped crazily in his mind, and he fought hard to stifle a wild laugh.

The urge to laugh dissipated at the introduction of a new, horrible image: Dad standing beside him, looking down at the brutally murdered body of Scott.

The vivid images kept resurfacing in his mind, blocking his ability to think with any kind of clarity. Had he just murdered Scott? He couldn't answer the question, nor did he have the time to dwell on it. He summoned whatever willpower he could find, nearly impossible, and he opened his door.

Dad stood in the hallway. "What were you doing in there?" He peered over Mark's shoulder, crumpling his massive brow.

Mark closed the door immediately and tried to maintain an expression of calm. "What do you mean?"

"I heard all kinds of noise," Dad said.

"I had a nightmare. I woke up and realized I was screaming."

"What was all that thudding and crashing? I heard some kind of crazy ruckus in there."

Mark struggled through a frantic cycle of excuses, but his fear kept resurfacing. *Think, think*, he told himself, but his nasty under-thoughts spoke louder: *Scott's dead body is on your bedroom floor, and you need to do everything you can to keep Dad out of there.* He slammed his eyes shut, as if physically urging the thoughts to vanish.

"Mark," Dad said. "What's going on?"

No empathy in Dad's voice. Dad knew something was wrong, and he was goddamned if he wouldn't get to the bottom of it.

"I lost my temper. I'm sorry," Mark said.

"Lost your temper. What are you talking about?"

"I flipped out."

Thin excuse, but it'll have to do. Just go with it.

"Flipped out?" Dad said. "What?"

Mark, speaking before processing, tried not to overthink his words: "I feel like everybody is accusing me of something. It's driving me insane."

"Well, you've got to talk to us about this stuff, buddy. It's no use not talking about it. You flipped out and what?"

"I threw some things around my room," Mark said.

"That's not a healthy way to deal with your anger, Mark."

Says the guy who throttles me when things go awry, Mark thought, but what he said was, "I know."

"Okay, so what's going on?"

Mark raised his arms in exasperation. "As soon as I got back from my suspension, I started getting all these questions from everybody," he said. "It's like everyone just *assumes* that I have something to do with this."

"Things aren't fair sometimes, pal. It's like I was telling you. Guilty by association. All that tough life jazz."

Mark promptly continued speaking, as if Dad hadn't even responded. "It feels like there's nothing I can do. I might as well fuck up, because it's what everybody expects, no matter what."

He found himself saying these words without consideration, a verbal stream of consciousness. It took him a few moments to realize that what he'd just said was true. If he was able to remove himself from everything that had recently happened (a near-impossible undertaking), he resented the way he was being viewed. He was sick of everyone assuming him to be the culprit all the time. No one gave him a chance.

No one, that was, aside from Madeline.

And look at how well you handled her marginal interest in your weird-ass self…

Standing in the hallway, dwarfed by Dad's stature, he thought of Madeline trying to pull him back into her house. The recollection probed. Wouldn't go away.

"Everything is falling apart," he said.

Dad looked taken aback for an instant, but then his posture visibly eased. He lowered to one knee and, just as if it was the most common motion in the world, he grabbed his son and held him. Mark pressed his face into Dad's shoulder. His father's sturdily muscled arms were shaking.

"I'm sorry I'm so fucked up," Mark said, and he meant it.

Dad squeezed him tighter, but the shaking didn't stop. Mark's vision was blurred into blackness against Dad's shirt.

The Shack is the answer. It had to be. He needed time. That was it, that was all he needed. Given the chance, he could uncover its secrets. He could find whatever he needed to find.

Dad pulled away and Mark looked at him through hazy eyes. He took the moment, an exception to life's rules, as an invitation to make his escape.

"Do you mind if I take a walk?" Mark asked. "I won't be gone for long."

"Where are you going? Maybe I can come along with you."

Dad's response, so shockingly out of character, took Mark by surprise. For several seconds, Mark was lost for words.

"I think I need time alone." Words with no connection to meaning. A recitation that could've been in a different language.

There was only one thing, one place, that had any trace of value left in his mind.

Dad looked momentarily offended before he forced a smile. "Okay, no worries…but let's all have dinner together in a couple hours, okay?"

"Thanks, Dad."

Further down the hall, Mom was peering through her bedroom door, partly ajar.

Dad patted Mark, walked down the hallway, and stepped into the bedroom with Mom. He shut the door behind him.

Mark waited a few moments, and then the shakes started. The terrible, exciting, overpowering shakes.

The time came, and he left. He didn't sprint this time, but rather, treaded softly and slowly: a futile attempt to ignore the horror, now steadily mounting.

The Shack loomed like an omen from the distance—dark, tangible. The darkness faded as Mark approached. Warmth replaced terror.

He pulled the door open, and he stepped inside. He now entered with the ease of a normal boy walking into a normal bedroom. Mark's real bedroom, after all, had become a haven for ghostly sounds, dead bodies, and monsters. The Shack, comparatively, was a sanctuary.

He spoke into the darkness, as heavy and oppressive as an unending sea of curtains: "Where are you?"

A chant began, a deathsong with neither melody nor rhythm: *kill kill kill kill…*

Mark stared into the shadows, searching for signs. Signs of anything. In this pure blackness, his other senses peaked: the kinetic force of soundlessness, the fumes of impossible age. Words crowded his mind, like smoky static, formlessly popping (*kill kill*). Mark tried to decipher a pattern, a clear method of discourse.

"What are you saying?" he asked. "What do I have to do?" He paused and, even through the fog, he found enough clarity to raise the question that needed answering. "Did I kill Scott?" He paused. "Was any of that real?"

Suddenly, the mental haze dissipated. In the space of an instant, he developed an acute awareness of his surroundings. Felt the stories sliding through the walls: a sense of safety, a sense of becoming.

Then a shaft of gray half-glow appeared before him, like a spotlight conjured by ghosts. The nightmare shape stood in the centre of the beam, just as it had stood before: still, silent. Mark stared into the light, which looked somehow dead.

"I need to know. Did I kill Scott?" he asked again. "Is he in pain?"

The Shack couldn't possibly be speaking, but Mark could hear it somehow: *...body can be taken, voice remains but body dissolves, only memories, only you/I/we, fading, no form no movement...* Pure malice burned in that nightmarish face, vacant sockets channeling the unthinkable. Mark had the sinking and terrible knowledge that these pseudo-communicative codes were directed at him. And just like that, his feelings of comfort disappeared.

He felt a feeling that might be described as weightlessness, but the feeling extended beyond the restrictions of such a physical term. It was a sense of suspension, as if he'd been picked up by some omniscient hand and was now being dangled over a massive void. He looked down where his hands should've been, and he saw that his hands were not there.

Of course. I can no longer feel them. Of course my hands aren't there.

The realization, so frank and lucid, brought a feeling of disbelief, and then an immediate, unhinged sense of horror. He cast his vision—did his eyes still exist?—further down. Where his feet should've been, there was only the gray-black floor of the Shack. No legs. No abdomen. Mark had lost his body. The inside of the Shack yawned below like an abyss, viciously open in its spatiality. The room seemed to invite him to step forward, knowing very well that he could do no such thing.

To be conscious, but not to be *there*... The concept hit Mark as he flicked his non-eyes frantically in every direction. He might go mad if this didn't soon end.

Or am I already crazy?

He would scream, but he had no mouth. Only his mind could scream, still enveloped in that otherworldly, static mist. He had the ability to survey, to rotate his visual plane as he would if he had a head. But he, Mark, as a physical being, no longer existed.

The nightmare shape appeared to delight in Mark's terror. Its hollow eyes gazed with vapid sadism, tracing Mark's invisible eyes as they scanned the environment.

Mark wanted to shout at the nightmare shape, to curse the Shack, to damn it to hell. Instead, he could do nothing but devolve into panic, a roaring force in the insignificant recesses of his own mind, where he was unseen and unheard. The Shack had taken both his body and his voice. Mark, a paralyzed consciousness suspended in space, tried to navigate the limits of his mind for a solution, an escape. Of course, he found none. What he found instead was a sense of total impotence, screaming incessantly in the nothing-space that he embodied.

...listen, you/I/we, do as I say, kill...kill...

Mark saw forms materializing behind the nightmare shape, exactly as they'd done the last time. Only last time, he couldn't help reminding himself, he'd had mobility. Last time, he'd possessed physical form, and a voice.

Soon, he found himself staring at Adam's dad. It couldn't really be Adam's dad, though. No, in the wake of unemployment, Adam's dad had shaped his entire limited existence into trips between the living room, the bathroom, the liquor cabinet and, on the rarest of occasions when sustenance ran dry, the liquor store. Nevertheless, this man had the precise countenance of Adam's dad: he was seated in an armchair, wine-fogged eyes fixed on a nonexistent television somewhere in the murk.

Mark saw himself standing behind the armchair. He was overcome by fiendish yearning for his own physical form, acne-scarred face and all.

He saw that Double Mark was holding a knife. Mom's favourite knife: Santoku, brand-new, multipurpose. Not only was he holding the knife, but wielding it. Preparing to use it for nastily suppressed inborn purposes. To maim, to injure, to kill. Mark understood the meaning of this scene: the Shack was preparing a demonstration.

He watched Double Mark stab, a single motion, driving the knife into Adam's dad. The handle protruded with grotesque rigidness from the base of his neck. Double Mark pulled the Santoku free, and a fountain of blood burst from the wound to paint his face. The harsh sound of metal scraping bone screamed across the room.

Adam's dad tilted forward, crimson rivulets coursing down his back, tremendous pumping geysers, like an image from some movie he'd watched a million times. *This scene would make even Tom Savini proud*, Mark thought crazily, but he knew all too well that this was no special effect. Double Mark wiped the blade on the chair and turned away, disappearing into the shadows of the Shack.

...do as I say...

Mark could not protest, could not conceive of anything save the intense need to possess his body again, to exist again.

He watched with bodiless eyes as the scene played out again, and again, and again, and again. He watched the murder so many times that he became impervious to its impact. He found his suspended mind drifting into unrelated territory, asking how long he might've been gone, asking what Mom and Dad were thinking right now. What was Madeline Fraley doing at this moment, and would he ever kiss her again? Would he ever get the chance to ask her if the rumours were true, that she scarred stars into her own legs? Would he ever get the chance to say that he was sorry for who he was, sorry that she'd suffered the misfortune of ever taking any interest in him?

Would he ever do *anything* again?

The scene seemed to play out for hours: blade punching through flesh, blood spraying, body slumping, and that final grinding, hideous noise as the Santoku dragged across a resistant ball of bone. Mark could not avert his attention or ignore the gory spectacle. Although he had vision, he had no eyes to shut.

Finally, after what seemed an eternity, the looped image faded. It dissolved into the blackness, leaving Double Mark and Double Victim tattooed on his memory. Mark cast his gaze downward, scanning for feet, scanning for body.

Nothing but air and floor.

He mind-screamed: *Please stop, please let me go, please give my body back to me, please please please.*

The nightmare shape stared at him. It moved its arms up and down with slow, exaggerated movements, taunting him with its ability to feel, its ability to *be.*

...listen, no time left, kill kill kill, kill or be killed...

Kill or be killed. Never had the Shack been so direct in its communication. Mark restrained his manic thoughts, wondering if the Shack somehow heard his floating mind. He tried to form concise sentences in his mind, sentences that might have the ability to set him free: *If you let me go, I will do whatever you want me to do—I will kill whoever you want me to kill. I have no choice. I can see that.*

Bodiless, voiceless, and terrified, Mark was almost unsurprised to discover that he meant every word he thought. When it finally came, the feeling of transformation was beyond anything he could ever hope to explain. For a moment, he experienced an utmost sense of empowerment; he *existed* again. He looked down and saw an oversized T-shirt hanging from his skinny abdomen, saw his twig-like arms, and rotated them, staring with awe. Yes, he existed again. Never had his slight and bony frame felt so heavy, so utterly physical.

The nightmare shape moved toward him. It held up three pale, slender fingers. Black sockets staring. Face inhuman, leering.

"Three?" Mark said.

The nightmare shape nodded.

"Three what? Hours, days, months, years?"

He heard the response with nerve-shaking clarity, wrapped in tingling, ghostly clouds: *. . . days.*

"Three days until what?"

He knew the answer even before asking the question: he would have to kill Adam's dad within the next three days. He knew this with certainty, just as he knew with equal certainty that the nightmare shape would torture him if he did not comply with its request. That it would remove his voice and his body again, and that, this time, it would not give them back.

Chapter 16

IT WAS WELL PAST 9 PM when Mark got home.

He entered the kitchen with caution and saw a note lying on the table. He recognized his mother's penmanship immediately:

Mark,
We were expecting you home for dinner tonight
Dad and I are not impressed
There is a plate in the fridge for you
Will discuss in the morning
Mom

"Fuck," Mark said.

In addition to the anxiety, terror, and exhaustion that grated his mind, he was ravenously hungry. He opened the refrigerator and saw his plate: chicken breast, white rice, and asparagus, all slightly squished by cling wrap.

He stuck the plate in the microwave for a minute, then ate his food, no care for taste or temperature.

There was another note awaiting him in his room. This one was written by Dad

Mark,
Thought we had a good talk earlier
Looks like we will need to talk about trust again
I love you but some things need to change
Might need to take away some of your privileges
Dad

"Fuck," Mark said. "Fuck."

He wished he had the ability to react with a standard, healthy sense of guilt. Instead, he felt only a sort of hollowness, impending. He was going to kill someone. He didn't know how or when, but he knew that he would find a way.

He dropped onto his bed, and he curled into the fetal position. He didn't even bother covering himself with his blankets. Maybe, true to the Shack simulation, he would need to put Mom's Santoku to creative use. She'd ordered it through a specialty retailer. She'd only just recently had it professionally sharpened.

He awoke early, a conscious decision to avoid a morning lecture from Mom. He wrote his own note and left it on the table:

Really sorry about last night mom and dad
Will explain later
Love you both
Sorry again
Mark

He didn't seek out Madeline or Adam when he got to school. He stood, lurking and destitute, on the outskirts of the field, until the morning bell cued his movement. For a moment, he considered avoiding school altogether. It didn't take him long to decide he had no better place to go. He didn't know if he would ever feel his old excitement for the Shack again, and even if he could think of anywhere else to hide, he rationalized that his parents would be contacted if he missed a class.

The last thing he needed was more trouble.

And so he went. As he crossed Ms. Corr's classroom, he felt Madeline's eyes. He did not look back, let alone offer the smile to which they'd both become accustomed.

After class, she quickened to a near-run in order to catch him in the hall. He tried to make his own brisk pace look natural, and he knew he was failing.

Madeline got ahead and stood in front of him. "You know I'm not mad about what happened, right?" she said.

"I know," Mark said.

"Okay, so why won't you talk to me, then?" Madeline asked. "Are you just being a prick or is there something going on?" She was nearly jogging in reverse to maintain her place in front of him.

He stopped moving and she gave him a grateful smirk, which he did not, *could* not, return.

"I'm talking to you right now," he said.

Madeline took a moment. Exhalation, frustrated and loud. "I just want to know why you ran away from me yesterday."

"I guess I got nervous," he said.

"Nervous about what?" Sincere in her voice, in her eyes.

"It isn't your fault," Mark said.

They shared yet another muted moment—awkward, shifting, fidgeting.

"Can we do something after school today?" Madeline asked.

"Why?"

"What do you mean, *why*? Because I want to see you. Is there something wrong with that?"

Mark's face heated up. He was conscious of embarrassment, of shyness, and somewhere in his mind, he was grateful for that consciousness, because it pushed away the dread that clogged his unconscious, even if only for a moment. During that expanse of time, perhaps a few seconds, perhaps a number of minutes, he was only aware of Madeline's eyes—emotive glimpses of ferocity, much brighter than his own.

"No, there's nothing wrong with that," he said. "There's something wrong with *me*. I'm sorry for being strange."

"It's okay, Mark, seriously." Madeline was staring, scanning. "So what's your final answer? Do you want to see me after school or not?"

Where else could he go? Home, where he would be chastised and scolded? To the Shack, which he now associated with a sickening sense of panic? Madeline's house sounded like the best possible option. And besides, he wanted to give himself another chance. Despite all the other chaos, he came alive with excitement whenever she was near.

"Yeah, okay," he said.

"Okay like you're being pushed into it or okay like you want to?"

"Okay like I want to. Like I really want to."

Madeline studied his expression for a few more moments, as if she expected him to go back on his own words. When she appeared to confirm that he was being genuine, she smiled.

***

Mark attended the remainder of the day's classes, oblivious to their noises, faces, and words. He thought only of the Shack, the Santoku knife, grim events with indiscernible outcomes. Whenever he managed to discipline his mind for the briefest of moments, he thought about Madeline, and he thought about her smile.

The day finished after a seemingly indeterminable amount of time, and he walked outside in a daze. As he stepped out the front door, he half-expected to see Adam again.

Adam was nowhere to be seen, but Madeline was there.

"How was your day?" she asked.

"I don't know," he said. It was the most honest response he could produce.

Madeline laughed the way she always laughed at him: not mocking or unkind, but shocked, disbelieving. "You don't know. Was it the worst day you've ever had? Was it totally amazing? What was it? It had to be something."

"I know," Mark said. "I mean, I know it should have been something. But it was nothing." He mentally reprimanded himself. Told himself to stop sounding so strange, to try and sound normal, at least partially normal.

To his pleasant or unpleasant surprise, Madeline did not laugh. "Weirdo," she said with a wan smile. "Just kidding. I've had those days, too."

They walked to her place, saying very little. As Madeline welcomed Mark inside, he again noted the dry, papery scent of used books, and the heavy smell of cigarettes smoked indoors. The aromas were already familiar. Comforting, even.

A woman called from another room: "Madeline, is that you?"

"Yeah, I'm here," Madeline replied. "Mark's with me."

"Who's with you?" the woman called.

"Mark."

"Who?"

"Mark." Madeline looked at Mark, rolling her eyes.

A few moments later, a woman walked into the entrance hallway. A half-smoked Camel was trailing smoke between her index and middle finger. She was using her other index finger to bookmark the paperback she was holding, something by Tananarive Due. She shook a stray lock of hair from her eyes, a gesture both simple and idiosyncratic, one that Mark recognized as inherited by Madeline. She looked around the same age as Mark's mom and dad, but Mark couldn't put a specific number of years to either of his parents, no matter how hard he tried to remember.

"Nice to meet you, Mark," Madeline's mom said. "I would shake your hand but, as you can see, my hands are full."

She didn't speak with the same calculated reservation that Mark had come to expect from grown-ups. It wasn't an *I'm Madeline's mother* greeting, but simply a person introducing herself to another person.

"It's nice to meet you, too," Mark said.

Madeline shifted her focus between the two of them, then gave Mark a long look. "Well," she said, "come on in."

Mark followed Madeline upstairs to her bedroom. It was much smaller than Mark's own, and also much more cluttered. The beige carpet was almost entirely concealed beneath a sea of clothing, comic books, makeup paraphernalia, deodorant sticks, and pens. Looking at the space between the closet and the bedside table brought an unwelcome flashback: the physical, nauseating sight of Scott's dead body bleeding all over Mark's carpet.

Madeline seemed to see the memory written on his face. She asked if he was okay.

Mark, feeling subliminally exposed, told her he was fine.

He forced himself into a space of psychological semi-awareness, wherein he could take control of his own voice and mannerisms. He couldn't let her see his fear again, whether suggested or open.

Madeline looked at him.

"I feel off sometimes, that's all," he said.

"That's okay." She reached out and touched the side of his face.

Mark had seen similar motions in countless films, television shows, advertisements; he knew the origin of the motion, even if he couldn't pin it to a specific moment or source.

He liked it just the same.

In one mad second, he made the decision to reveal the source of his dread. To partially reveal it, at least. "The cops have been to my house," he said.

"What? Why?" She didn't remove her hand.

To Mark, her hand seemed somehow protective, and his inhibitions began to skitter away. "Because Scott's gone. They think I had something to do with it. My parents don't trust me, either. I can tell." His words sounded, to himself, like they were half-formed, disjointed.

"I'm sorry, Mark," Madeline said. "That whole situation just seems really awful. They still haven't found him, have they?"

"No, they haven't."

Madeline's touch drifted from his jaw; she reached down and took his hand, locking fingers. "Come here," she said. She led him toward the bed, sat on the edge and pulled him beside her. "It sounds like things are really bad right now. I get that."

"Thank you, Madeline."

"Don't mention it."

"This whole thing is sort of... How can I say it? It's sort of specific," Mark said, "but at the same time, it isn't specific at all. I mean, sometimes I don't know what exactly is happening. What it *is* that's scaring me."

Madeline's smile, unassuming. "Honestly, I don't know what it is you're talking about, but I've had some really bad shit happen in my life. Shit that I've had to deal with."

"Yeah?"

"Hell fucking yeah."

"Like what?"

Madeline flicked her eyes around the room for a long time, then looked back at Mark. "People dying. And not dying in the normal way. Not, like, dying in a bed because they were old or had a disease or something. People dying in bad ways. People I knew, people in my family."

Her speech, staggered, reminded Mark of his own nervousness. "What do you mean?" he asked. "What happened?"

Madeline bit her lower lip and shook her head, gently.

Mark spoke up: "I mean, if you don't mind my asking."

"It's so fucked up. Why am I talking about this right now? How does that happen? You talk about one thing and then something else comes up and before you know it you're talking about—"

"What?"

"Really fucked up shit."

"You don't have to talk about it if you don't want to."

She shook her head. "We're already talking about it... I mean, it's just that I feel like I understand what you're saying...in some way."

"You do?" Mark said.

"Yes," she said. "It was my cousin who died. She was a little kid. Nine years old. You probably saw it on the news or heard your parents talking about it."

"I don't watch the news."

Madeline gave a small nod.

"Was she..." Mark began, and stopped himself. He experienced a moment of inability, of necessitous inaction, the impossibility of speaking without committing violence. "Was she killed?"

Another small nod.

"Were you two close?"

Nod.

"I'm sorry, Madeline. What happened to her?"

Madeline dabbed her eyes with the bottoms of her sleeves, hiding tears before they could surface. "She was taking the bus home from school, one of those yellow elementary school buses. There was this guy…this older guy who lived alone. He worked at some call center, it turns out. Never married, had no friends. Apparently, he'd been following my cousin for a while. Her name was Monica. My cousin. Anyway, he followed Monica for a few months. At first, he would watch her leave from his living room window in the morning, then he would watch her get off the bus in the afternoon. Just watching, you know…to begin with. The police say that he had memorized her routine by the time he…by the time he did what he did. Eventually he got braver, and he started watching her at the bus stop bench. He just kept getting closer and closer, and nobody seemed to notice… He was only some frail middle-aged guy, you know. Glasses, clean-shaven, turtleneck sweater. Then, this one day, he finally grabbed my cousin and took her into a public park. It was in the winter. Nobody goes there during the winter. It's surrounded by houses, but I guess nobody took a look out their window and noticed that something strange was happening. Nobody saw this fucking creep with my cousin. So he took her there and he…" Tears. Harsh, wracking, assaultive tears. Headache tears.

Mark, peeling away from his own paranoia, was shocked for a moment. He wrapped his arms around Madeline's shoulders, and he squeezed, gently. Pain, a new form. He squeezed harder, harder, fighting the urge to begin crying himself.

"I'm sorry," he said.

"The worst part is, Mark, that her parents always asked me to walk her to and from the bus stop," Madeline said. "Her parents both worked full-time, you know, and they really trusted me with Monica. It would've been no problem. She only lives a few houses over, but…oh, fuck."

"You don't have to talk about this," Mark reminded her. "You really, really don't."

Madeline seemed not to hear him, continuing to speak: "I told her to pretend that I walked with her every day, and she was so sweet. She just told her parents that I did it, and they never doubted it. They both worked from fucking 7 am to 6 pm every day, so how would they ever know the difference? I just wanted to walk alone. I didn't want that fucking, I don't know, that responsibility, I guess… I lied, and I made her lie, and now she's dead."

"I'm so, so sorry." He said it because he knew that, at this moment, it was the thing he should say. And he *was* sorry, but the words were far from effective, far from achieving the impossible.

Madeline's crying subsided gradually. Her lips, wet and salty with tears, crushed his own. He closed his eyes.

This was a kiss.
This was normal, and this was right.

Chapter 17

IT WAS PAST TEN WHEN HE finally left her house, and the street was now fully darkened. His obligations resurged in his mind, chewing his nerves to shreds. By some force of will, he would need to go home and find a weapon. He would need to make his way into Adam's home, and he would need to kill Adam's dad in secrecy.

He would need to find a weapon, and he would need to kill Adam's dad with it.

No matter how many times he ran through the scenario in his mind, he could not imagine it in any remotely logical way. His brain was an empty room.

He tried to lay out his plans as he walked: First, he would sneak into his own house, avoiding his parents altogether if possible. Second, he would get the knife from the kitchen, or maybe find a blunt instrument from Dad's toolbox, or maybe both. Finally, he would walk to Adam's house and…

He would work out everything else when the time came.

When he got home, he saw, to his dismay, that there were still lights on. Even more concerning, that fucking squad car was again parked in the driveway.

He opened the door. What other choice did he have?

Mom, Dad, and Thompson were sitting at the dinner table. Familial positioning.

Just thank Christ it isn't Selby sitting there.

Mom's face was red, tear-streaked. Dad and Thompson were talking in quiet, serious tones: Men of Authority tones.

Thompson, then Dad, then Mom came to attention at the sound of the door. They rose to their feet in unison.

"I know it's late," Mark said.

"You're not leaving this house again," Dad said. "Not until we tell you to leave. You are to stay here and go to school. Nowhere else."

"Mark, we don't know—we didn't know what to think," Mom said.

Thompson stood behind them, his expression bearing an uncanny resemblance to Selby's default scowl. "Now that he's home, I can call off the search." He looked at Mark. "You've got to keep your parents posted."

There was an angle in Thompson's tone, one that Mark could hear clearly. Thompson knew, somehow, that Mark was involved in Scott's disappearance. Yes, Thompson was now on Selby's side. Good cop passing as bad cop, or vice versa.

"I'm sorry," Mark said. "I was at a friend's house. I lost track of time."

Dad blew air between his teeth. "Lost track of time."

"I did."

"Know what goddamn time it is?" Dad turned to Thompson. "Thank you, officer. Sorry for wasting your time."

Thompson, pulling on his boots, gave Mark a look to match the angle of his voice. "I'll leave you folks to it, then. Your parents were scared, Mark. You shouldn't be out at night without telling them where you are." His utterance, superficially kind, was full of hidden meanings, full of threats. He looked at Mark: predator eyes. "They might think the worst. They might think you're up to something." With that, he gave Mark's parents a final nod and stepped into the darkness.

Dad began yelling the moment the door was closed: "Get to your room. I'm sick of this crap from you."

Mark abided. While, in the past, he was always frightened by the sight of his father's fury, it now seemed mild, perhaps even comforting, in comparison to the real gravity of his situation.

As he walked upstairs, he heard Mom talking to Dad: "I would appreciate if you would let me talk to him, too. I didn't even get to say anything before you started shouting."

"I wasn't shouting," Dad shouted.

"Oh, please," Mom said. "I can never get a word in edgewise."

Mark closed his door and flopped on his bed, facedown. His parents continued arguing, their exchanges escalating in volume and intensity.

"I'm under a lot of goddamn stress and—"

"—just forget it, I don't want to talk about this anymore and I—"
"I'm getting *real* tired of the way things are around here."

"That's easy for you to say. You're the one who gets to do all the talking while I—"

"I'm not in the mood to talk about it anymore. Conversation's over."

There was the sound of Dad's steps, heavy and aggravated. Mark heard his father pause outside his door for a moment, audibly fuming. Then, mercifully, Dad crossed the hall to his own bedroom, shutting the door behind him.

Mom came up the stairs a few minutes later. She knocked on Mark's door. "Mark? Can I talk to you? Please."

As she stepped into the room, Mark noticed that her face was scrawled with fatigue.

"I'm sorry," he said.

"You can only say you're sorry so many times."

"Well, I don't know what else to say. I *am* sorry."

"Then why do you keep putting us through this?"

"I'm not trying to put you through anything," Mark said. "Things just, how can I say it… Things just *happen* to me. They happen and I accept them."

"Things happen to you? What are you talking about?" Mom leaned in to inspect his eyes. "Have you been doing drugs?"

Mark couldn't help but notice the routine nature of this exchange: every remark sounded familiar, something he'd memorized through unconscious osmosis. He tried to focus on Mom's fear, tried to focus on the emotion of her words.

"No, Mom, I haven't been doing drugs. I've never done drugs in my life," he said, truthfully.

His honesty must have been convincing, because the distress began to visibly ebb from his mother's face. "What is it, then?" she asked. "Why do you keep disappearing? Why won't you listen to us?"

"I met a girl, Mom. I like her a lot. I was spending time with her and I didn't notice how late it was getting. I'm sorry. I am."

He selected his words with great caution. Thoughts of unthinkable violence, of the Shack's faceless face, kept gnawing holes through the utter banality of this conversation.

Mom looked relieved by his explanation. "Okay, Mark. Just keep us posted, okay? Please. That way we don't have to worry." She didn't move from the doorway. Her fingers floated down to her wedding band for a moment before falling back to her side. "What's she like?"

How do I describe someone like Madeline Fraley to my mother? How do I describe her to anyone?

"She's nice," Mark said. "What can I say? She's really nice. Do I have to talk about it tonight? I'm tired."

"No, you don't have to talk about it. I'm sorry. I'm just being a mom. You know. I'm really glad that you met a girl, Mark."

A silence fell between them, and Mom took her cue.

"Get some sleep," she said. "We can talk about it tomorrow."

She stepped out of his room. As soon as she left, Mark began mentally mapping his night. When he took a moment to reconsider his options, he had a paralyzing flashback of his mind suspended in space: the inability to move, the inability to speak.

He looked down at the bedside table. Ribbons of flesh stuck to smears of drying blood. Gore on the carpet.

Could his parents not see this? Was he hallucinating it all?

He couldn't risk the belief that he was.

"Okay," he said, speaking to the Shack, or the nightmare shape, or whatever was listening…wherever it was. "I'll do this thing."

'This thing' meaning murder.

He shuddered, turned out his light, and sprawled on his side, eyes on the alarm clock. He watched the time pass, the shift between one minute and the next, never forgetting the Shack for a single moment, never forgetting the threat of permanent nonbeing: the disembodied terror of losing himself.

He watched the clock until 12:15 am. A new day.

He stepped into the hall and saw that the lights were off in his parents' bedroom. He made his way to the kitchen, found the biggest handle in Mom's knife block, and tucked the Santoku into the waist of his pants, cold steel kissing flesh.

No time to dig through Dad's toolbox.

As he exited his house, he kept reminding himself that he had no choice. This had to be done.

He had no choice.

***

Mark walked the streetlit suburban sidewalks between his own house and Adam's, the knife tap-tap-tapping his lower abdomen. Entering Adam's cul-de-sac, he made the subconscious observation that there'd seemed to be no space of time between departure and arrival.

His entire walk consisted of maddening, hypnotic reminders: *I have no choice… This has to be done… I have no choice…*

The lights were off in the house's front area. He crept around to the side. Bluish, electric TV light flickered from the living room, illuminating the hunched shape of Adam's dad, large, sedated, cradling drink #25 or 26 while ogling a bad monster movie. Bowing to his gods.

Mark edged back around to the front of the house and made a futile effort to open the door. Twisted the knob and found, unsurprisingly, that it was locked. He attempted to build a mental plan, ignoring the terror and adrenaline that now coursed through his body. He mentally highlighted the unavoidable physical barriers that would get in his way: Adam's dad was a heavy and brutish man. A man capable of lifting his oldest son over the bannister and holding him there for minutes on end; Mark had seen it happen. Mark couldn't give Adam's dad the chance to see him, no, couldn't allow him to process exactly what was about to happen.

Going to have to take him by surprise, Mark thought, and his subconscious added nastily, *Like a fucking coward.* He forced himself to ignore the thought.

It was very important that he not allow anybody to see or hear what he was doing. He would have to do it quickly. He would have to do it out here.

He remembered the murder-vision to which the Shack had subjected him. In the vision, he'd stabbed Adam's dad in his armchair. Did he need to perform the act exactly as it had been depicted in the vision? If so, he couldn't possibly do it tonight, or for that matter, he probably couldn't do it on *any* night. Not if he had any intention of getting away with it.

How do I do this? How?

Questions for silence, addressing entities that could be anywhere, everywhere, or nowhere.

No reply. No fog voice permeating his thoughts. Only the hushed night, crisp and black.

He looked at the door. He was blocked out. He couldn't fulfill the vision's exact criteria without breaking in, and he had no idea how to break into a house. Not only that, but breaking in would also make too much noise and elevate the risk of his being seen.

He arrived at his previous conclusion a second time: he would have to do it out here. *Do it* meaning he would have to kill Adam's dad, to murder him with Mom's favourite vegetable-chopping knife, out here.

He staged the situation in his mind. He would knock on the door and hide.

Where? He made note of a shrub under the front window; that would need to do. When Adam's dad stepped outside, he would lunge.

He would go for the throat and he wouldn't, couldn't, think twice.

He cursed under his breath, stepped up to the door and pushed the doorbell. He jumped off the step at the sound of a *ding-dong.* He crouched in the shrub and drew the knife. Held it close and high, ready to pounce.

He heard Adam's dad muttering inside: "Who the heck?"

The voice was yet another reminder of what he was about to do, and who he was about to do it to. This was the man who was always offering him secret beers, talking to him about old horror movies and girls.

This was his best friend's father.

He heard footsteps. Slow, plodding, beer footsteps.

He gave himself a terse mental reminder: this was also the man who Mark had seen brutalizing his wife, the man who drank far, far too much, who hurt—no—who *tortured* his family, who liked to break things, who liked to feel powerful by making others feel powerless.

The door cracked open.

"Hello?" Adam's dad said. A clumsy shuffling of feet. A pause. A shuddering intake of breath. "Ah, the childish pranksters of the world."

Mark's instincts flared as the door began to close. He made a hissing sound between his teeth.

"Huh? Who's the—"

Mark cut off Adam's dad midsentence, or, more accurately, the knife cut him off midsentence as Mark slammed it into his calf. Mark felt the impact, felt the depth of the blow; a muscle twitched and pinched against the blade, sending reverberations up into his hand. The muscle seemed itself a microcosm of Adam's dad, a feverish and panicked thing that resisted pain with horrible intensity.

Mark used all his strength to pull the knife free.

Adam's dad howled and crumpled into himself, clawing at the wound with lager-sticky fingers. He'd been reduced to infantile squirming and wailing within seconds; at the other end of the mortal thread was senility—an entry into death. Mark recognized this as the gruesome defilement of life's trajectory: ultimate destruction. Blood poured, a wave painting the doorstep and trickling into the shrub, making pitter-patter sounds against the leaves, like a heavy rainfall. Mark could smell it.

Instinct took reign. No time for morbid reflection; no time for anything. He grabbed the man's ankle and pulled, his fingers wet and warm with blood. Adam's dad tumbled in three directions at once, his head connecting with the doorstep, his hands clattering against the door frame, his lower body slipping into the shrubs. "Oh fuck oh Jesus what the fuck is going on oh Christ," he rambled, his speech liquefying from a combination of alcohol and probable brain damage from the fall.

Tears ran down Mark's cheeks, hot animal tears. He wiped them with his left hand, his right hand coated in red.

No time to think, he reminded himself.

He stabbed, and he stabbed again. He tried not to see the human form in front of him, tried instead to remember the creature from his bedroom, fanged and snakelike.

Muscle, thick and hard, resisted the jabs. The man's fingers scrabbled weakly at his shirt.

Mark raised the knife high over his head and brought it down in a swift, final blow. There was a gut-flipping squelch as the man's throat opened.

Then, Adam's mom from inside: "What's going on?"

Mark fought the overwhelming urge to vomit. Averted his eyes from the body, from the person he'd just killed.

How quickly Adam's dad had transformed into a dead body…

Mark ran away; the return of the sprint, even faster than he had used to run toward his original Shack visits, when he couldn't fathom a quick enough arrival. His destination was the same now as it had been then, but all the excitement was far gone.

Chapter 18

PURE ADRENALINE.

Mark collapsed, rattling, in front of the Shack, his eyes closed.

The Shack stood silent. Gray, indifferent.

Mark opened his eyes, allowing for a sliver of vision. Blood caked his arms in scabbing rivulets, the Santoku handle was smeared red. The smell of murder was all over his body.

Disgust bulldozed his senses, and he stood, swaying and quivering.

He made his way to the Shack and pried the door open. What was once reverent, euphoric, even holy, was now only a door.

Once inside, he sprawled on the floor.

"Okay, okay, it's done," he said. "What a night." Laughter. His own or someone else's. "What is wrong with me?"

He couldn't feel the Shack, nor the nightmare shape's presence.

He experienced his aloneness, suddenly, as something of great magnitude: nobody, nothing could rectify what he had just done. He was splattered with blood, dark and pungent and real.

"Help," he said.

His words were greeted with all the significance of a quiet cough. He shut his eyes again, an effort to reclaim this space as his hideout, his secret, his sanctuary.

All he could feel was the blood, slowly scaling patches on his flesh. His mind screamed *help* in an unbroken stream, but he said nothing. He stared into the gloom and he was overcome by useless recollections of his early visits: acerbic nostalgia, the sense of Scott and Adam beside him, fragments of exchanges, the taste of tobacco. The elation he'd once associated with the Shack itself.

He shunned the memories, brought himself back to the moment, sick and isolated and streaked with gore. The Shack had made him do what he'd done tonight. If anything could still help him, it would be the Shack. He reclaimed the power of his first experience and applied it to the moment. It was a strained and mechanical and ultimately impossible process, but he focused intently nevertheless.

"You," he said, setting the coded phrase in motion, initiating the ritual. "I..." The words were heavy, blunt, and awkward. Tonight's trauma was etched into every moment. "...We."

He slipped, invisible, into a strange place, a place that hearkened the moment before a powerful spell of *déjà vu*. The white fog crept into his mind, ensnaring words and images that he claimed as his own. He embraced the misty static, allowing it to slip between his innermost terrors, to envelop his brain in a ghostly placenta.

The nightmare shape was here. He couldn't see it, no, not yet, but he could feel it now.

There was a flash of the familiar, of the deathly light, and a moment later Mark was facing a figure, but it wasn't the expected shape. It wasn't the tall thing that he now recognized and knew. What he saw was much more petrifying. What he saw was himself.

It was not a simulated version of himself. It was not the projected-future-Mark that he had seen before. This was a complete, physical, and *true* duplicate. Mark didn't know how he was able to distinguish between this Mark and the simulation Mark he had seen in the past, but he *knew*.

Mark Two advanced.

"You're tricking me," Mark said.

He expected a fragmented, semi-conscious voice in response. He expected Shackspeech. Instead he was met with a clearly audible vocal response: "This isn't a trick."

"I'm not falling for it. This isn't me." Mark raised his knife as Mark Two drew closer. "Stop moving. For Christ's sake, leave me alone. I did what you told me to do."

Mark Two pressed forward until Mark was backed against the wall, wielding the Santoku, no intention established.

"Who said it ended after this?" Mark Two asked, reaching into the waist of his jeans to draw his own knife: same brand, same bloodspots.

"This isn't real and you aren't tricking me and I'm not killing anyone else," Mark said. Fear welled physically in the back of his throat, solid and cold, like frozen fruit.

Mark Two took two more steps, until he was inches away from Mark. Mark smelled the blood spattered on Mark Two; he felt Mark Two breathing on him.

"Listen to me," Mark Two said. "I am you, for all intents and purposes. If you do not do as you are told, I will go out and report you/myself to Officer Selby and I will destroy your/my life. You have no choice but to listen to me. Do you understand what I'm saying?"

Mark shuddered. Did not respond.

"Good," Mark Two said. "Now listen. You'll have to kill again."

The word *kill* triggered panic.

Mark lunged, but Mark Two grabbed his knife arm and squeezed his wrist. A pinching pain forced Mark's fingers open and his Santoku clattered to the floor. He swung with his other hand, but Mark Two grabbed his fist mid-swing.

"Don't fuck around. It's a waste of time," Mark Two said. "Listen to me. You'll have to kill again. There's no way around it."

Mark's head sank, his chin against his chest. He let his arms go loose and Mark Two released him.

"Who?" Mark asked. "Who do I have to kill? How long do I have to keep doing this?"

"You have to do this as long as you're told to do this."

"Who do I have to kill?"

"Do you remember that fat fuck who was always giving you trouble at school?"

"Clinton." Mark shook his head, frantic. "No. He's my age. He's a kid. They'll catch me."

"Don't worry. You don't have to do it yourself this time. You won't have to feel his windpipe burst under your hands." Mark Two laughed. "It'll be easy. Just bring him here and we can take care of it."

Mark took notice of the word *we*. Was the Shack comprised of multiple bodies? Multiple identities? Was Mark speaking to a version of the Shack at this moment? He set the questions aside, deciding that they might just push him over the precipice that cast sanity into the depths of insanity, a precipice that drew closer and closer, seemingly, with every moment.

"I can't kill Clinton," Mark said. "He's a kid. Adam's dad hits…*hit* his wife and his sons. I did what I had to do, but I can't do this. Clinton's just a kid."

"This isn't a discussion," Mark Two said, his voice toneless. "You know what will happen if you don't do as you're told."

Mark experienced a flash of disembodiment, a replica of that previous torment. For the space of a second, he was stripped of his body and his voice. He sensed the removal, like some intangible surgery. His body was returned to him with equal immediacy.

With the quick return of his voice, he begged again: "No, please."

He cast his eyes toward the gray, dust-coated floor. Peaks of nausea twisted his gut, hot currents, and he doubled over. He puked, tainting this once-sacred place with the stink of his bile.

"Please," he said. His mouth was sticky with vomit acid.

This time his appeal reached no visible listener. Mark Two was gone. The Shack was empty again.

Mark's mind was still shrouded in the crackling, foggy whiteness of something's presence. He turned to the door and he considered running home. It took him less than a second to realize he could do no such thing. Going home would only bring him closer to his parents' suspicion. They would see him covered in blood…or would they? They didn't seem to notice the monstrous fluids covering his bedside table. Still, he couldn't risk taking the chance. If they saw him right now as he saw himself, they would make inevitable connections, and he would be at the mercy of their moral judgments.

The solace of the past was the prison of the present. Mark ran his exchange with Mark Two through his mind, searching for loopholes, which he unconsciously knew he'd never find. He slouched against the wall and thudded his head against the wood: once, twice, again, again. He began to appreciate the budding of a blunt pain in his skull. He swung his head one final time. It connected hard enough to sting and throb.

He stared into the darkness, and he did what he knew he had to do: he tried to set out yet another plan for himself. Another plan, which would take him even further from his own humanity.

As hard as he tried to focus, no ideas would come.

When it had come to killing Adam's dad, he'd had the advantage of speed and surprise. If he had to lure Clinton to this place and get him through the door, he would need to take a completely different approach.

He entertained the morbidly absurd image of bludgeoning Clinton upside the head and dragging his colossal body, block after block, all the way to the Shack. He snorted, a sound dry and empty. *I can't do this by myself.*

The Shack was as silent and impregnable as ever.

***

Mark squinted into the blackness. For a few delirious moments, he was convinced that he was safe inside his own bedroom, that he'd just awoken from some long and uncanny dream.

The feeling passed as soon as his nostrils sucked in the Shack smell. And mingled with the scent of dust and ancient stories, he inhaled the metallic stench of stale blood. Coming jaggedly to his senses, he realized that he was splayed across the floor on his back, that his spine hurt like hell, that his shoulders stung, and that his mind, pulling threads of memory from every direction, was enveloped in Shack mist.

"Fuck," he said, forehead aching.

He must've fallen asleep mid-thought. He sat up and pressed his palms against his temples, tried to imagine what he might look like right now. After putting his imagination to work for a second, he decided against pursuing the thought any further. He needed to leave. He couldn't do what was required of him while he was still in this place.

Half-memories swirled around the crux of his pain. He had to find Clinton.

"Fuck fuck fuck." Hissing, massaging his head.

He found the door, and he pushed it open. Sunlight, hot and yellow, seared his eyes. His head protested. Mark had never been drunk, but he imagined a hangover might feel something like this. As he stepped into the field, the fog unveiled from his mind, and his headache intensified, the pain all-consuming. He entertained the short-lived thought that he was dying—caked in the blood of his victim, his brain short-circuiting in his skull as he adjusted to the sunlight.

If he went home, he would probably be seen by his parents, not to mention the police. However, if he avoided his home, he would be putting himself at risk by walking around in these clothes. He tried to imagine Ms. Corr's reaction if he were to walk into her class, filthy with gore and dead-eyed from pain.

School was no more of an option than the police station. He decided he would need to go home and change his clothes, no matter the risk.

He stuck to alleys and isolated streets as often as he could. A couple cars slowed down to accommodate swivel-headed looks of concern.

One of these people will call the police, Mark deduced.

He was running out of time.

He had a moment of relief when he got home: the driveway was bare. His parents were probably driving around looking for him, or maybe they were at the police station filing reports and providing information. Shaking their heads and saying, "Where did we go wrong, what happened to our son, please help us find him."

Mark opened the door with caution, stuck his head inside, then followed with the rest of his body. He made his way to his bedroom and, as he extended his arm to open the door, he was reminded that he was still covered in a maroon layer of blood. He turned around and rushed into the washroom. He went straight for the sink. The blood looked even redder in the white bathroom light. Technicolor vivid.

He laid his arm under a stream of hot tap water and the scabs melted into liquid, reborn as scarlet streams that dribbled down the drain and splashed the sides of the basin. He was taken aback by the sheer *amount* of blood. Glancing into the steam-fogged mirror, he realized that the blood was also smeared all over his face, his neck, and his collarbones. His own appearance was even more frightening than the sight of the gore. Uglier than usual today.

He would need to take a shower.

He ran through a list of concerns, fragmented and frantic. Showering would take time. Changing his clothes would take more time.

His parents wouldn't be away from home forever.

He tried to focus on the moment, to mechanize his actions; he needed to carry out his plans in a very specific way. He needed to avoid thinking and, more importantly, he needed to avoid panicking.

He turned on the shower, hotter than hot. He dropped his blood-smeared clothing in a heap and stepped under the hissing spray of water. It felt good to be scalded. Grimacing and red- fleshed with heat, he was able to forget about the Shack for a period. He took the quickest shower he could manage, watching the water that dripped from his body as it transitioned from crimson to pink to colorless.

After drying himself, he inspected the towel for bloodstains. He had a moment of paranoia as he looked at the blank white fabric; what if his parents found the freshly dampened towel? This was unwanted evidence.

He rushed into his bedroom and hid the towel under a pile of dirty laundry, struggling into the cleanest looking T-shirt and jeans that he could find, his ears pricked for the sound of opening doors and footsteps. After dressing, he stood by his bedroom door and listened closely for any sounds. Once satisfied, he ran down the stairs. He reached the front door and reconsidered; if his parents were pulling up at this moment, he'd be fucked.

In fact, what if the house was being watched? What if the police were hiding somewhere at this very moment? His brain was overrun with these frantic possibilities, hysteria on a rampage. *Okay, okay, calm down, calm down.*

He turned abruptly and made his way to the back door. As his fingers closed on the handle, he heard the front door opening. A steady stride followed, the unmistakable sound of the Mom-walk. He twisted the handle and noticed, hysterically, that it was still locked. Mom's footsteps grew louder. Closer.

He wrenched the lock and shut the door behind him. *Oh God, oh God.*

Mom might've heard the sound, but Mark didn't have the time, nor the option, to find out one way or another. He eyed his surroundings for unwanted observers. He couldn't see anyone, but that was no comfort to him. The stillness was alarming, the vacancy suspicious; not to mention, Mom might be heading straight for the door to find out whether she'd imagined the sound of its closing.

He ran through the backyard, hunched like an old man suffering intestinal pain. People must be looking. Everyone would know he was missing by now. He pushed awareness into a corner, focusing instead on his next destination. On Clinton.

Clinton would be at school today, and he didn't have many friends. Mark would probably be able to confront him alone.

The first objective, as always, as Mark continually reminded himself, was to avoid being seen. The second objective was to move Clinton from the school to the Shack. He considered taking the bus to school, but quickly changed his mind. Too public. Too open. Walking was his only option.

Time existed differently from any form he'd ever known: a buffer between one bleak alternative and another. He arrived at the school around 2:00. Classes didn't end until 3:20. He found a spot to hide near the school doorway and waited. Time passed, but Mark didn't feel it passing. He could never have enough time.

The sound of the bell announced the end of the school day, ushering him into the present, away from his schemes, half-formed and impossible.

He waited a few minutes, watched the school entrance from his vantage point. The doors crashed open and a surging crowd pressed out, a wave of laughter and semi-audible exchanges.

Mark watched closely, his viewpoint limited. He saw Madeline exit with two of her friends. Talking. Smiling. He swallowed hard, tried to ignore his stinging eyes, forced himself to look away. When her voice was no longer audible, he turned his attention back to the door. He might have missed Clinton.

Shit. He clenched his teeth and began grinding them together, the trickle of bodies condensing, condensing. *Where the fuck is he?*

Mark raised up a little to watch the disappearing crowds. He couldn't see a single body big enough to be Clinton's. *Clinton must still be inside.* Either that, or he wasn't at school today. Mark pushed the second alternative into his mental periphery, gritted his teeth until he thought they'd snap right out of his gums.

An uncountable amount of time passed, and Mark started pacing on the spot, no longer concerned with being seen. Now he was concerned about the possibility of not existing.

What if he couldn't get Clinton to the Shack?

"Shit shit shit sh—" He cut himself mid-curse as Clinton exited the school, opening the doors without enthusiasm, heavy arms hanging at his sides, eyes cast groundward. Even from this relative distance, Mark could see tears shimmering on Clinton's cheeks.

Was this guilt that Mark felt?

Clinton began to shuffle, heavy-footed steps and intermittent sniffles.

Mark glanced around to see if anyone was watching. Once he'd decided that he was in the clear, he came out from his hiding spot.

"Hey, Clinton," he said.

Clinton turned to him.

The plan in motion. There was nothing Mark could do now.

"What're ya… What're ya doing here?" Clinton asked.

Clinton took a few steps back. Mark took note of the body language. *He's nervous. You're going to have to take this very slowly*, he thought, and paused.

"Well, I wanted to talk to you," Mark said. "Can I do that? I mean, I wanted to apologize."

Clinton's features became a cartoonish montage of reaction: cynicism, doubt, anger, reluctance, fear, hesitation. "I heard people saying there's something wrong with ya," he said. "I heard 'em saying that your buddy disappeared, that there was a lot of shady stuff going on."

"What kind of shady stuff? I don't understand."

"The cops have been asking questions," Clinton said. "*Real* police officers. They've been at the school and the principal keeps calling kids to the office."

For a moment, Mark registered the sheer strangeness of this conversation. If he'd been told a few months ago that, in due time, he would be standing outside the school unveiling personally related murder conspiracies with Clinton, he would've burst into hysterical laughter.

"Well, I don't know about any of that," Mark said. "All I know is that I want to apologize." He employed a flat tone, tried to imbue as much empathy as he could muster. He felt like a slaughterhouse worker hushing an animal before slicing the innards from its body.

"Why apologize now? Ya could've apologized a million times. I never even see ya."

"I guess I've just been thinking about it a lot. Listen, do you smoke?" Mark asked.

Clinton looked simultaneously excited and terrified. He stared at Mark and, absentmindedly, he wiped his eyes. "Honestly, I've never smoked before. We can't smoke on school grounds, though. Especially not after fighting. They'd kick our butts right outta school."

"Yeah, I know, but I figured we should have a smoke together," Mark said, "just to make things up, you know?" He paused. "You're right, though, not here. There's a cool place I was thinking of going."

Luring the sacrificial lamb, leading him to the slaughter.

"My mom would kill me," Clinton said.

Now that Clinton was actually considering this, Mark's guilt—yes, it was guilt—hovered like a shadow on his mind, underlined every thought, made his stomach broil with unease.

"She wouldn't have to know," Mark said. "You can walk off the smell. Chew some gum and you'll be fine. Honestly."

"I guess I just never expected ya ta talk ta me. Unless ya were telling me ta go ta hell or something."

"Well, all that's over now," Mark said. "I feel bad, I really do. I hate what I did. I hate the things I said. I want to make it up to you." For a moment, he feared that all this guilt would turn to a river of bile and spill out his mouth. He gulped.

Clinton smirked. He was so fucking flattered by the invitation. "All right, sure. What the hell. Where would we go, though?"

"It's this rad place I know," Mark said.

"Is it far?"

"No, it's not very far from here at all. We could walk, easily."

"What is it?"

Mark remembered his friends asking that very same question when they'd first faced the Shack. In that moment, they'd all felt the way that Mark imagined Clinton must feel now: cautious, thrilled, and completely ignorant.

"It's a shack," Mark said.

"A shack? People live in shacks. I can't break inta someone's house or anything."

"No, no. It's nothing like that. Nothing like that at all."

Clinton stared quizzically.

"It's abandoned," Mark said. "Nobody lives there."

Clinton's face became a process of visible shifting, of the awareness that this conversation was truly unusual. "How do I know you're not messing with me?"

This is taking too long.

"Messing with you? No way, man. I want to make it up. I wouldn't pull anything on you. We both know you could kick my ass, anyway. You're five times my size."

Clinton laughed. "Yeah, sure, I could kick your ass, but what if you have five other guys waiting in this place?"

"Clinton, I don't even know five other guys well enough to do something like that. Plus, I don't want to hurt you. Honestly. I just want to smoke a cigarette and make amends."

Clinton, reluctant, gradually dispensed with suspicion. "Yeah, all right," he said. "I'm in. So where's this place?"

Mark couldn't decide whether he should accept his own nauseating tension or be relieved by Clinton's acceptance. He chose to do the very thing that had motivated him since the Shack had first taken control of him: he didn't think about it.

"Come on, let me show you," he said.

He was constantly mindful of being seen as they walked toward the Shack. Whenever they strayed from the sidewalk and into an alleyway, Clinton gave him a cautiously inquiring look.

"It's a shortcut," Mark said repeatedly.

Clinton looked introspective as they reached the edge of the field. "Look, man, I forgive ya. I mean, what ya said wasn't cool, the joke, I mean, but I'm over it." He sighed, blinking back oncoming tears. "And being angry and sad won't bring my dad back ta life."

Words so frank and naked, so abrupt, that Mark was at a loss for a response.

"What did I say? What was the joke that set you off?" Mark asked. "I honestly can't remember."

Clinton began to speak, then clapped his hand to his mouth as if he were trapping the tentative words inside. "I can't remember either," he said, after some time.

They looked at each other for a moment and burst into laughter. Clinton was laughing at the absurdity of the whole thing.

Mark was laughing in horror.

After a minute, Clinton stopped laughing, but Mark couldn't stop. It was like some sickness was coming through these powerful, body-rattling hysterics. His jaw ached, and his cheeks burned.

He finally took control of himself.

"Are you all right?" Clinton asked.

No, Clinton, I'm not all right. Truth be told, I'm pretty much completely fucked up.

"Yeah, I'm fine," Mark said. "It's just really funny."

"Yeah, I guess so," Clinton said. "It's not *that* funny, though."

Mark chastised himself. He'd better not screw this up, not now that he had made it so far.

"You got the cigarettes?" Clinton asked.

Mark had anticipated this question, and he provided a rehearsed response: "Of course, but we can't smoke them out here. I don't want to get in shit."

Clinton nodded with the kind of grim affirmation normally reserved for surgeons and FBI agents.

Mark chuckled again, then quickly stopped himself. "All right, let's go."

As he walked toward the Shack, its presence struck him more powerfully than he could recall in recent memory. It was no longer just a building, but something... What was the word? Transcendent, maybe? He could sense it again, even from the expansive distance across the field. The hairs on his arms were raised.

Clinton puffed behind him, struggling to keep up. "Hold up, man. Holy crap, ya running a marathon here or what?"

Mark didn't slow down. He continued forward, and noted pleasantly that his guilt was now gone. The Shack's warmth was back. Only now, it wasn't just sewed into the walls of the Shack, but dancing across the field. Trickling into everything.

Mark reached the Shack. He absorbed all its majesty for a moment, momentarily forgetting his duty. Now, there was only Mark, the walls, and the secrets within. He forgot about Clinton. How did he keep forgetting what the Shack was capable of giving? How, and why, did he keep losing this sensation?

Clinton's voice broke the pleasure of the moment. "This is it, huh? What is it, some kind of a storage shed or something?"

"Yes. Something like that. Do you want to go inside now?" Mark said.

"I don't know. This is pretty weird ta me."

"What's weird? I've been in there hundreds of times. We can just hang out and smoke some cigarettes."

The Shack's presence was now palpable, even hot. Mark perspired, that staticky white fog beginning to cloak his mind.

Clinton looked over his own shoulder. "I don't know, man."

"There's nobody here," Mark assured him. "It's just us."

Clinton shook his large head, Scott-style. "All right, screw it. Let's go in."

A jolt of energy shot inside Mark's skull, as if the Shack fog was blasting his synapses. He reached for the side of the door. Pried it open.

"It's dark in there," Clinton said, concern reappearing on his face.

"Of course it is," Mark said. "Don't worry, there's a light switch in there." Hackneyed improvisation; it would have to do.

"What? How? Where's the power source? What is this place?" Clinton took a step back.

"It's a shack. Come on, let's have a smoke."

As Clinton slowly retreated, the Shack's allure began transitioning, shifting. Something menacing began to sing a tune in Mark's mind. A chorus of hissing voices told him to do it now, chanting *you/I/we you/I/we you/I/we you/I/we*, until he could think of nothing else.

Mark seized Clinton's thick forearm and held it with a vice grip. Time for the less tactful methods of Plan B. "I'm not fucking around," he said. "Get in there."

Clinton struggled. "What the hell're ya doing? Let go of me."

Mark pulled hard.

Clinton didn't budge. "Are ya crazy? Let me go, I said. What the hell's wrong with ya?"

Mark pulled harder, and Clinton swung with his free hand. A bundle of knuckles clouted Mark above the ear, prompting a shrill frequency that pierced his head.

The pain gave him strength. "Get in there, you fuck," Mark said. He yanked as hard as he could physically manage, and Clinton toppled to the ground with a diaphragmic *whoof*.

A shadow of remorse probed through Mark's fog-stricken brain. He was about to take this kid's life.

The thought, or the idea of the thought, was quickly washed out by Shack mist. Quickly enough for Mark to act.

Clinton, still flat on his back, tried to hoist himself to safety. His fleshy arms spun like propellers in reverse, pulling away from Mark.

Mark advanced, combat mode, oblivious to consequences. He looked down at Clinton's broad, pleading face and he did what he had to do: he stomped. Clinton yelled at him to stop, and Mark liked the sound of his desperation.

He stomped again.

White light veiled his vision, occupied his body with potency and unreality. He stomped until he heard the crunch of a breaking nose, like the sound of a radish crunched between molars.

Clinton was still. Mark became suddenly aware of the blood flecked all over the sole of his sneaker, sprinkling the bottom of his pant leg, covering Clinton's face and chest. The sight of blood was no longer shocking to Mark. He accepted it as the product of his vocation.

He searched his surroundings and determined that there was nothing nearby. Nothing and nobody.

Here was safe.

He hunched down, and he seized Clinton's limp arm. He kept his guard up in case Clinton still had some fight left in him, but the kid didn't budge. Mark had kicked him into unconsciousness.

Or worse.

Mark tugged and got nothing but resistance. He was trying to move a giant.

"Jesus Christ," Mark said. He became conscious of the sun. Sweat stuck his T-shirt to his chest. He swore and fumed until, mercifully, the Shack fog wiped his stress.

He pulled again, dragging Clinton two inches, maybe three. The strain was incredible.

Mark looked over his shoulder. The entrance to the Shack was four or five feet away.

Staring into the darkness of its open entrance, he realized how much it looked like a mouth. He didn't shiver.

He pulled. Clinton budged. Mark pulled again. He released Clinton's arm in exasperation, and it dropped to the earth with a resounding thud. Mark squatted over Clinton's waist, wrapped both arms around the boy's fleshy midsection. Clinton smelled like sweat-smeared deodorant, blood, stale fear.

Mark pushed the limit of every muscle in his body, yanked and cursed and yanked. It wasn't easy, but the big fucker was starting to move. Mark stumbled in reverse until he could feel the Shack's musty warmth, gusting from the blackness and hissing against the back of his neck. They were nearly inside. His mind was a cloud of crackling whiteness. Something human swimming in a tumult of beautiful nonsense.

He made his way into the Shack, and he collapsed backward. Clinton's head hit the floor with a grotesque *whap*.

Mark sat panting and wheezing, eyes fixed on the unmoving body before him.

He'd done it. The kid was as good as dead. The *kid* was as good as fucking *dead*.

The Shack's door pulled itself shut, and the bang was powerfully startling. The nightmare shape was making its presence known.

Mark heard breathing that didn't sound like breathing, that sounded more like thumping, a blunt and heavy noise…the closet noise. The sound whirled around him in an aural cyclone.

Clinton twitched and gurgled. He emitted a low moan through half-parted lips, like a child resisting demons in a nightmare. Only this wasn't a nightmare, and Clinton was not going to wake up.

…bring prey, you/I/we, task done, watch gore sucked inside the body, spat on walls in glistening patterns, the shape of your nightmares…

Mark could hear it, could hear the Shackspeech. He uttered a strange sound, a sound very similar to Clinton's half-dead moan. The Shack fog was clearing again, scattered by remorse, evaporated by fear.

"Do you have to do this?" Mark said. "Isn't Adam's dad enough?"

He received no response. The thumping continued. Clinton's chest rose and fell, rose and fell, the blood blot on his chest spreading and contracting accordingly, a sick and deadly rhythm.

This was a murder.

This was happening, and it scared the shit out of Mark.

He tried to take his mind someplace else, into abstraction beyond experience, into some realm that could lift him from this hell. Nothing came to mind but the gurgles and screams of Adam's dad, the sound of puncturing flesh, the pervasive, unceasing sight of blood, fountains and rivers and magma-like remainders.

"Stop," Mark said. "Please stop."

The sound magnified: thump, thump, thump.

"Let him go. He's a kid. You can't take him. I brought him here, isn't that enough?"

The thumping.

"Oh Christ oh God this is happening oh fuck oh fuck oh fuck."

The thumping, the thumping, the thumping.

Those thumps created a vibrating frequency in Mark's arms and chest, shivering his bones and his organs: that feeling of standing too close to the speakers at a concert, when the music assaults the body. Too much sensory input; too much experience.

Clinton came to, his wet eyes blinking at the blackness. He touched his face and jerked at the discovery of blood on his fingertips. "Wait… What… Mark…"

Mark slid away, further into the darkness, trying to stifle the sound of his own breathing.

"Hello?" Clinton said. "Stop messing with me. What's going on?"

The Shack burst into a floodlight wash of brightness. Clinton screamed. Mark shielded his eyes with his forearm.

The nightmare shape stood before them, towering, static, unfeeling.

"What…what is it?" Clinton said.

Mark wanted to apologize, wanted to say something. Anything. But he couldn't speak, and instead he found himself laughing again, a horribly painful laugh that made his stomach hurt.

The nightmare shape moved, a morbid and somehow graceful drift-walk toward Clinton. The thumping continued, punctuating Mark's laughter with teeth-rattling volume.

Clinton was now sitting, cross-legged and wide-eyed, staring up at the nightmare shape with an expression of total unknowing. He continued fumbling for the beginning of a sentence, but nothing would come. "Mark… What… I…"

Mark laughed harder; he laughed until the contents of his stomach probed at the bottom of his throat, until he could taste the remnants of his most recent meal, and he found himself suddenly trying to recall the last time he had eaten, trying to identify the origin of the puke-marinated lump that bobbed inside his esophagus, and the mere thought made him sick until finally he submitted, spraying vomit in a staggered and putrid stream. It pumped and coursed from his mouth with the timing of his laughter; he coated his jeans and his shirt-front and the floor. He laughed harder, vomited again.

The nightmare shape advanced.

And advanced.

Clinton was screaming now. Mark could hardly hear him through the din of his own mirth. When the sickness finished flowing from his body, he stared into the light: a dead, impenetrable whiteness.

The tall, drifting silhouette moved closer to Clinton, and Mark was hypnotized by the fluidity of its movement, a smooth and effortless levitation over the dust-caked floor, which seemed somehow worlds below. As Mark stared, his body flowed, becoming motion; it took him a few moments to realize that his perspective of vision had shifted. He was now drifting, staring down at the shuddering and frantic pink mass that was Clinton.

He looked toward the wall and he saw himself, saw his own awestruck face, motionless but alive. It didn't take him long to realize that *he* was now the nightmare shape and that, aside from rotating his head, he could not control his movement. He was floating closer and closer to Clinton, as if he was on some grisly conveyor belt.

He saw the raising of his long and somehow weightless arms; he saw skeletal, probing fingers drift in front of his vision. *His* skeletal fingers.

He wanted to scream, but couldn't. Mark, his body in the corner, was laugh-crying, his vomit-speckled lips a hideous contortion. But he was trapped in this relentlessly moving thing, and he was now directly above a howling, wet, blood-spattered Clinton. He felt an inexpressible power, the ultimate surplus of bodily and mental input; the mist that enveloped his brain was now enclosed around his entire body, not only encasing it, but oozing into it, flooding his pores, his receptors, every cellular microcosm of his being. He was omniscient, the overseer of everything. The scenario before him ceased to exist.

All that he felt, all that he saw, all that he was, was dead light.

He was the indifferent but all-powerful energy that guided not only his own narrative, but all narratives; he was the stories in the walls of the Shack.

Perhaps he embodied this form for two seconds, perhaps he experienced it for a decade. Time was impossible. There was no periphery, no background information.

And then it ended.

Pain, body and soul, oh fuck it hurt, pain shooting up his thumbs and into his hands, the veins in his neck pulled taut like cords. He quickly discovered the source of his pain: he was gripping, squeezing Clinton's thick neck with all his strength, plunging his thumbs into the flesh.

He knew immediately that Clinton was dead. Mark looked, dumbfounded, at Clinton's teary and orb-like eyes, cast upward, permanently subservient to the forces that had sucked the life from him.

Mark pulled his hands away. This wasn't the agreement. He was only supposed to bring Clinton to the Shack. His role as murderer was not part of the deal.

He shouted into the darkness, nonsense lamentations. His screams were tiny, shrill, and irrelevant, and the darkness ignored him. He jumped back from Clinton's dead body, blood everywhere, his hands throbbing from the strain of a stolen life, nightmares and impossibilities roaring across his mind.

He ran for the door without allowing a moment for reason, then halted as soon as he closed the door behind him. He stared into the infinite green expanse of the field, and it only took seconds to realize that he had no place to go.

He was quickly awash in the violent red memory of murder.

He remembered Selby's sternly scrutinizing face; that bastard would take one look at the body of Adam's dad, and he would know.

Mark stared across the field to survey the suburbs. Everything he feared was there, in those houses. Suspicious moms and dads waiting by the telephones, waiting for a glimpse of the young killer.

He entertained the possibility that nobody would suspect him, but the possibility could only stand up to reason for a millisecond. All it took was the recollection of Adam's hysteria to put things into perspective. Even if nobody else had any reason to believe that Mark had killed these people, Adam would set them straight.

Adam would send them after Mark.

Then again, Mark had done everything the Shack had told him. He had no reason to submit himself anymore. He could see and feel that he no longer needed this place.

But they would all know. They would find all the evidence he had inevitably left behind. How many people had probably seen him with Clinton? How many observers had seen him wandering the streets in these bloodstained clothes?

He had no choice but to turn back, and so he pried the door open. The Shack's musty air blew into his face. He nodded, a submission to fate, and he re-entered.

The floor was bare. Clinton's body was gone, but Mark still felt the thickness of his resistant flesh sending pain through his fingertips. He closed the door and sat on the floor. He couldn't sense the Shack's seductive pull, although he badly wanted it. He stared into the darkness, trying to ignore the throbbing, now insistent, in his hands.

He fixed his gaze on the shadows that obscured the walls, an effort at extraction, a groping for narrative, a sense, lingering somewhere in there.

A pang stabbed his guts. Was it hunger? Was it more nausea? Anxiety, maybe? Or rage? He couldn't decipher between feelings anymore.

He pushed the physical sensation away, wedged it into his mental background, and focused again on the shadows, trying to urge the Shack into showing him something, telling him something, into being there when he told it to be there.

Agony demolished his focus. He swore loudly and relented. Curled on the floor and sucked dust into his slow-breathing nostrils.

Maybe it was because he fell asleep. Or maybe he didn't fall asleep. Or maybe he was dreaming. Or maybe he woke up.

Whatever the reason, the Shack spoke to him again.

White light sliced through his closed or half-closed eyelids, scorched his vision and seared his mind. The power, as always, was insurmountable.

He scrambled to his feet and shielded his eyes from the brightness.

...stand frozen, lean over the edge, tremble and scream, closer to dissected dream...

"You. I. We." Mark's bones buzzed with otherness, electric; as he spoke the words, he knew that they were good, and he knew that they were right. The meaning of the dead light shifted in his mind, and his pain subsided along with the shift.

This light was powerful enough to do whatever Mark wanted. He cast his eyes down to his gore-soaked shoes and his quivering hands, his mind drifting in the ether of something else, something better.

Maybe his body was the thing that was holding him back.

"Take me somewhere," he said, with no consideration for the meaning.

The light didn't brighten, but intensified, throbbed, pulsed. His flesh tingled, bumps standing on his forearms, then surfacing along his chest, his stomach, his legs, his groin. His penis severely stiffened. He could feel the light caressing him, bleeding into him: white heat. The light fizzled and flowed like a bad television signal. Mark stared into it, water beading his unblinking eyes.

The light brightened until he believed he might be staring at the sun. He gasped, inhaled energy. The light maintained full exposure until Mark wasn't sure he could take it anymore; then, in increments, it began to dim.

He thought the light might be coming to life, that it had reached its zenith and was now taking the form of something that lived, breathed, and moved.

What it was really doing was changing; not just changing, but reimagining. The confines of the Shack were a memory. The light was giant, the way Mark used to imagine God when he was told to recite *Our Father* before going to sleep as a boy; a vast and indifferent power that was everywhere and everything. This light, though, was broadening, now even larger than the God that Mark had imagined as a young child. Mark saw the walls drifting away, specks on the uncharted or nonexistent horizon. The light smeared every corner of his vision, like an endless cinema screen. Infinite blankness, white. He was paralyzed for a few moments.

Then he took a step, his body filled with heat.

It wasn't until he moved that he realized the floor was gone. It wasn't a matter of what he could feel or not feel; no, not that at all. Rather, whatever he'd been standing on was no longer there. In its place, there was only light and warmth.

And so he moved.

And the whiteness was something else; the whiteness was another place, and he kept reminding himself that there were no walls, no roof, no floor. At this moment, there was no Shack.

The thoughts of bloodshed faded, finally seeping into his unconscious, where he no longer had to confront them.

And he was on a road, and the road was formed from shoe-stamped dust instead of asphalt, and the only thing lining the road was a stretch of unmarked grass, late-spring green. The smell was stronger than anything.

And so he moved.

And the road kept yawning before him, and he kept advancing, but all he could see was the road and the grass.

He wanted it to be something else.

And so it was.

It was a path toward something specific; this path belonged to him.

He walked until the novelty of unbridled movement was no longer appealing. He stopped and turned to look behind him; the path appeared to stretch into infinity both ways. He stepped off the path and onto the grass. It was springy and light under his shoes.

He walked, the green field lifting at a slight incline. He enjoyed the effort of ascendance, not knowing what might be at the peak, what might be on the other side.

Eventually, the ascent levelled out and he could see something in the distance. He was too far away to distinguish any details, but it looked to be about the size of an adult human being. Whatever it was, it didn't move.

He assigned the shape as his destination.

The details revealed themselves as he approached; not only was it the size of a person, it was the shape as well.

Drawing nearer, he wondered if it was indeed a person. It was standing still, possibly surveying the environment.

"What are you doing here?" Mark asked. He was closing in now.

He was mere yards away when he was able to take in the person's physical details. It was at that moment that he discovered it wasn't, in fact, a person at all; it was a statue. Sunlight glinted off the smooth, stony surface of the sculpture. It was made in the likeness of a man, although Mark could not yet make out the face.

He finally reached the statue. Detailed musculature, like something he might see in one of Mom's coffee table art books. Mouth twisted down, pulled open, the appearance of a scream. The eyes wide, extremity through the flatness of stone.

Mark no longer thought this was a statue. No, this looked like a person encased in stone: Gorgon prey.

He looked over his shoulder, in the stony man's eyeline. Did the stony man, the statue, *have* an eyeline? Mark and the statue stared together, either in autonomous singularity or unison, at the sky, powder blue, smeared with wisps of cloud.

Mark could not see whatever was at the bottom of this hill, and so, adrenaline speaking, he decided to descend and find.

At the bottom of the hill, the field of grass was broken by a thicket of trees. Unlike the grass, these trees looked as if they were living their last days before a chilling winter: sparse, paper-dry leaves hanging from branches, trunks like weather-beaten granite.

Mark could not see beyond the trees, could not even see through them. They were grown together in a thick wall: gray, knotted, withered.

Inspecting the trunks more closely, he was reminded of the Shack's walls. Was this an illusion? He suffered a paranoiac vision of himself staggering through the blackness of the Shack, his dumbfounded face pressed against the wall.

Was this really just a wall? Was he still inside the Shack?

Uncertainty as a tugging. He knew he would have to enter the thicket in order to validate or invalidate his suspicions.

Turning sideways, he wedged himself between two of the trees. For a moment he was caught against one of the knobby trunks and he thought, *This is it. The illusion ends here.*

Branches scraping his arms, he strained forward, until finally he broke through the trees. Once he'd made his way through, he found himself facing more tightly clustered trees, probably barricading yet another layer, or fifty, or an unending procession. Dim and creamy light seeped through the tangle of branches above.

A sense of urgency, fear as undercurrent, drew him further into the forest. He swiped branches away from his face, snapped dry sticks and tossed them aside. He walked long enough that he began to expect an emergence, to expect another side, but the forest only grew thicker. It only grew darker. The creamy light dimmed, curdling, becoming gray.

Unease simmered beneath his curiosity, but he pushed it away. There might be something to find in this forest.

Gray went black.

Something threaded in the wood.

Maybe if he could just listen closely enough, rise above his own thoughts, he would be able to hear what the trees were saying. And so he stopped.

And he listened.

...the sound is so loud it scares you, lost in sight of a savage apparition, escape alone to order of images in painted torture, the closing vortex burns, lineage of sacrifice, centipedes born from a storm as you scream, the sound is so loud it scares you, vital centre repels the horror of weakening control lines, a sacrificial image as the thing comes toward you, the axis of that screaming fragment begins to breathe, you envision modern artworks where codices step forth, wish to kiss the horror as half-spent suction is found, yes, this sound is so loud it scares you...

And as the space got tighter, as the trees got thicker, the voice or voices or voicelessness got louder, and when Mark listened, when he strained to hear, he could make out his own voice within the dialectal wash: a symphony of hisses and whispers and half-formed prophecy. This was not *a* narrative; inside the forest, here and now, was *the* narrative. This was what he'd been waiting to hear. He couldn't discern whether his eyes were open or closed, whether he was asleep or awake, but whatever he was, wherever he was, he was listening.

Gradually, the words began to appear, physical, palpable, in his mind. That is, instead of sensing or hearing the signs, he could see them, thin lettering that scrawled through his sub- or unconscious. The writing thickened and darkened, like the sky's strangled light, and it began to expand. And soon the words were something else, soon the words were objects, soon the words were their meanings.

He thought the word *rat*, or rather, the word *rat* came into his thoughts and, a moment later, something tickled his calf, something light and bristly, like the tip of a frayed and overused toothbrush: a rat's whiskers. A bead of wetness touched him a moment later, like a warm, damp, bobbing grape: a rat's nose.

He cast his eyes down to see the thing hunched at his feet, its beady eyes staring as it sniffed at him.

He jumped back and the rat screeched dully. The word *rain* brought a sudden torrent upon him; signifiers, animals, feelings, sounds bombarded his thoughts. Things alive and abstract began swarming around him, skittering, overwhelming, the unthinkable given form.

As he stepped over wriggling masses of arachnids, breathing intuition and filth-streaked fur, a new word rose above the din of his mind. A name:

Madeline.

His heart might've skipped three beats when he saw her there, standing before him, maybe four feet away, and she was not the spectre of Madeline, not a replica of Madeline, but Madeline herself. Her eyes widened with terror. A quiet sound rose in her throat as she stared around at the chaos of shapes and things.

She had not yet seen Mark and, for a moment, he did not want that to change.

He said her name quietly, almost to himself, and she heard it.

She turned to look at him, and her fright turned to terror in an instant. She screamed so loudly that Mark's first instinct was to clap his hands to his ears.

She continued screaming as Mark ran toward her.

He only advanced a few steps before his foot was caught in a tangle of damp, furry rats. He stumbled and fell facedown. He called out to Madeline, wanting to ask her how she'd got here, still not knowing where *here* was.

He recoiled from the wet, hotly breathing face of a rat that was sniffing at his face. He managed to scramble to his feet. Madeline, motionless, had stopped screaming, but her look of terror had deepened.

She was looking at something behind him.

And whatever it was, it had horrified the voice right out of her.

Chapter 19

MARK DID NOT WANT TO TURN, oh God, that was the last thing he wanted to do, but he wanted to stop it, whatever it was, from coming any closer. He wanted to stop it from reaching Madeline.

The Santoku. The thought filled him with greater terror: the weapon was not with him. As his fear mounted, hideous aberrations piled his mind, a revolving door clogged with catalogues of grisly stalkers, ghosts, monsters, diseases, faces, and the faceless.

Madeline's voice returned, and it returned as a scream.

Mark pushed himself to focus through the mayhem, and he turned.

He wasn't facing the motley crowd of beasts, both human and inhuman, that he had expected; instead, he saw a giant, frail and ashen man—was it a man? was it even human?—shuffling slowly toward him. The face was gaunt and sickly, sharp cheekbones protruding through flesh the colour of distant storm clouds, its body impossibly thin, somehow thinner than a human skeleton. It took one shaking step forward with a leg longer than Mark's entire body, reaching for him with lesioned and flaking arms.

Its eyes effaced its candidacy as a human form: black orbs that bulged through caving sockets, unreflective and unfeeling, like those of an overgrown insect. Tight, gruesomely colorless skin tightened and pulled back from the place where lips should have been, stumps of teeth chewing at a swollen purple tongue, which leaked puslike liquid in foamy streams.

The thing took another step, and Mark heard Madeline begin to run away. He imagined an axe in his own hand, the kind that Dad brought on camping trips for chopping firewood. Obediently, the weapon materialized; one moment his right hand was empty, and the next the weight of the wooden handle pressed into his palm.

The hideous creature took in a humid, gusty breath, followed by a pus-flecked cry. Mark could smell the inside of its mouth, the scent of badly rotted meat, human blood and waste.

It took another step, and Mark froze for a moment, thinking that this thing was too big, too powerful, that there was no way he could take it down. Instinct kicked in, and he swung.

The axe was sharper than he'd expected. He caught the thing in the middle of its unfathomably long shin, cleaving bone with a single stroke. The monster hissed and tilted to one side, leaning all its weight on the spurting remains of its chopped leg. Globules of whitish fluid fell from its mouth, splashing Mark's head and shoulders, stinging, scorching small holes in his flesh. He could smell his hair burning.

The monster swiped with one gargantuan hand, closing tendril-like fingers around Mark's abdomen and lifting him into the air. It began to squeeze. The force was extraordinary, and Mark could immediately feel his bones straining from the pressure. He screamed, hacked at its fingers with the axe.

Colourless blood sprayed in geysers, soaking Mark's face and body. Its grip began to relent as Mark chopped again. Half of its forefinger dropped to the ground, squirting and twitching. The thing released its grip, and Mark thudded to the ground, tumbling.

The thing curled like an ant in flame, limbs jittering, eyes staring without staring, moaning and shrieking. Mark didn't want to risk letting it regain its strength, and so he ran at it, full speed, bringing the axe over his head. He slammed it into the creature's stomach. Yanked it free. Attacked again.

And again.

Flesh split, then tattered. The ribcage cracked and exploded in a flurry of pallid bone fragments. Mark dodged the enormous, clawing digits. Monolithic innards spilled onto the grass, steaming and pungent. The thing lay in a heap, writhing, ruined hands clutching at the air.

Mark ran to its side and stared down at its vast, grotesque face; its eyes were the size of his head. He saw his reflection inside one of those inky, thoughtless globes, saw steam rising from his own gore-soaked body, saw rage and panic in his contorted expression, and he wondered how monstrous he must appear to this abominable thing. It clenched its grisly, uneven teeth, flesh pulling back to reveal sore-riddled gums.

Mark wielded his axe for the final swing. He emitted a cry so merciless that he frightened even himself, and he struck the creature in the middle of its papery-fleshed forehead. The axe landed and quivered between its eyes, streams of blood spilling, brain matter like cooked oatmeal coating the ground. Its black eyes stared consciously one moment, and unconsciously the next.

He had killed it.

He stepped back, waiting for it to move again, prepared to attack. He wheezed ragged, painful breaths, his skin red and terribly itchy.

The thing did not move. Mark wheeled around, searching for Madeline.

What he saw instead was a damp and squirming mound of rats beneath clouds of concepts both concrete and abstract, manifested in ways that could never be translated into language, but that Mark now saw plainly and vividly with his eyes.

He tried to concentrate, tried to tune out the sights and smells and sounds that had appeared with such immediacy and ferocity. He tried to envision the thick, scrawling font in his mind again. Tried to will it into shapes that he could control.

He focused long enough to imprint two words in his mind: *Madeline's house*. The words became objects and he was standing in her living room. The space was cigarettes, molding pages, and silence.

And Madeline's mom was calling Madeline's name. Mark quickly realized that Madeline was not there with him. He was alone in the room.

And so he thought. He thought her name: *Madeline*.

The word clattered in his mind with a tumult of memories: her spiky belts and bracelets, her smile, the way she hurt, the stories she'd told, the sound of her voice. Mark wondered suddenly, crazily, whether he could bring back Madeline's cousin, little Monica, simply by envisioning her name. Could Scott be returned from wherever he'd gone?

Incantatory words, an absence. He was standing in Madeline's living room, filth falling from his body and puddling around his feet in a gray blotch.

And Madeline's mom was descending the stairs.

Frantic, Mark bolted. He heard Madeline's mom running down the remainder of the stairs.

"Matt, I mean Mark," Madeline's mom called to him. "Wait a minute."

Mark was already out the door. He was running; he was out in public. People could see him. As he sprinted down the block, he imagined all the suspicious suburban window glances. He imagined all the assumptions and possible phone calls.

He ran until his breath felt and tasted like burning blood.

***

Warmth stroked him, inside, as he entered the Shack.

He imagined Madeline's mother running down the sidewalk; he imagined all the terrible things she would think he might've done to her daughter, and he cringed, slumping against the wall.

He inhaled darkness, and he tried to calm himself. Heard the voice: *...you/I/we, one more life, one more, have your body, one more life to have your life...*

Mark regrouped, caught his breath, processed the voice.

He knew what was being said, what was being transmitted, that he would have to kill again, that he had no choice.

"Who?" he asked, utterly withdrawn.

The whiteness condensed and collapsed into itself; hot, wispy motes curled and spun in the centre of the room, casting shadowed spirals against the walls. Nonmatter becoming matter, smoke taking shape.

Madeline was standing before him. He took one look at her smile and *knew* that she was not the real Madeline. Not this time. The real Madeline actually smiled; the shape in front of him was only gracing him with the impression of a smile, the impression of humanity.

His throat clogged. He waited for the figure to expand, to elaborate, but the artificial Madeline stood, isolated and resolute. Staring at him.

Smiling.

"No," Mark said.

...the voice, the living guts burst by a jagged plea, the breaking of a sound so loud it scares you, do this or...

"I can't. No. Not Madeline."

Horror encroaching on the outline of his own defiance, the impending fear of realization. His protest was thinner than air.

"I can't and I won't," he said, louder this time.

Yes, he'd protested on both previous occasions, and on both previous occasions he had carried out the task presented to him.

But this was different. This was Madeline and he would never do it. Never, never, never.

With the speed and frequency of a strobe light, he was stripped of and replaced with his body and voice. He looked down and watched his hands disappear, appear, disappear, appear, disappear, appear.

He screamed and the sound came out in stutters, silence in his moments of nonbeing.

The Shack was reminding him what it was willing to do. Not only could it take away his life, but it could transform his life into an approximation of hell. To exist, but not to be there.

The strobing stopped, and Mark had his body again.

"I won't."

...*kill kill kill kill kill kill kill*: the chant battered his mind, beat his logic, assaulted his protests. A throbbing, rhythmic pulse of white light accompanied the word, searing eyes and flooding body, the electric sense of something with extraordinary power.

"No. I won't. No."

Something moved inside the wall, something immediately to his right, something that struggled hard enough to shake the wood, and in turn, to shake Mark as well. Mark tried to maintain the appearance of resolve.

The wood crunched, and a thin crack scrawled up one of the planks; a neon bright glow oozed through the slivers.

"No." His body shook, thumps rattling his skeleton, shooting spasms through his fear-tensed muscles.

The nightmare face appeared, not inside the room with him, not even in physical form, but rather casting a white outline, blazing, around his thoughts. Penetrating resistance and imprinting every impulse with pure, hot, sickening fear.

"No. Fuck you. Go to hell. No." He might have said the words, or they might have drifted, thin and wraithlike, from the crack in the wall.

The crack spread; the white light bursting through was interchangeable with the faceless face now closing like a claw on Mark's mind.

He thought of screaming. He thought of every frightening image in every frightening film he'd ever seen. He thought of the anxiety caused by unlocked doors, the body-locking paranoia of hiding from the predator, the animal dread of being hunted, the sick and lonely underthought that he would die, that all names and addresses and spoken words sifted quietly through an infinite and indifferent turnstile, that the notion of a great beyond was romantic drivel masking impenetrable blankness.

He thought of words, and he could not speak them.

Chapter 20

MOM PICKS UP THE PHONE MID-RING; a smoky tail wisps from the cigarette in her other hand.

A baited sigh seems to rise from the very walls, the room now pregnant with parental anxiety.

Dad is on the sofa, indifferent to Mom's smoking, his eyes foggy and directionless.

Mom takes a long pull on the cigarette before speaking into the phone. She speaks through a white plume of nicotine: "Hello?"

"Where'd he go?" Dad mutters. "Oh God, what did we do? What have I done?"

"Honey, please, I'm trying to listen to this," Mom says, and she takes another drag. "Hello, I'm sorry. You're Madeline's mother? I don't think I've ever met Madeline."

"I want to strangle my own son," Dad says to no one more than himself. "Or hug him. Oh God, maybe both."

"Honey, please. I'm so sorry, miss. How long has she been missing?" Mom asks into the phone. The cigarette falls, still smoldering, onto the carpet. There has never been an ashtray in this home.

Dad reaches for the phone, unsteady on his feet. He hasn't eaten in almost ten hours.

Mom moves away. "I can handle this, honey," she tells Dad. Then, returning to the phone call, she asks, "Did you say you saw him at your house? When?"

"Who is it? Let me talk to her," Dad demands.

Mom plugs her free ear, and Dad slumps back onto the sofa, rubbing his glasses uselessly on the bottom of his shirt.

"You followed him?" Mom asks the woman, who has called to set their world even more off-kilter than it already is. "Did you find him?"

Dad gets up again, glasses tumbling from their perch on his stomach. "Where is he? Who are you talking to?"

Mom ignores him so that she can listen to Madeline's mom. "There's a house in a field? I'm sorry, I don't understand.

"Did someone do something to Mark?

"A shack? What do you mean?

"Did someone do something to my son?

"Maybe we should all go together and look," Mom suggests to Madeline's mom. "I'm so sorry for all this. I know how you feel." She sets the phone down and makes a deliberate turn to face Dad.

His eyes are alight with tentative violence. "Who was that?"

"Did Mark ever talk to you about a girl named Madeline?" Mom asks.

"Never," Dad says. "What's going on?"

"That was Madeline's mother on the phone. Apparently she's been missing for several days as well."

"What? Did Mark have something to do with it? How many goddamn kids were involved in this?"

"I don't know," Mom says. "Her mother told me that she followed Mark and he went into a… What did she say? Into a house or something."

"A house."

"Yes, in the middle of a field."

"A house in the middle of a field? What the hell is that supposed to mean?"

"She said it was a shack."

"A shack."

"Yes."

"Did she follow him in?" Dad asks. "Where's Mark?"

"She said it was empty inside."

Acknowledgments

This book has evolved a lot, taking several different forms and passing under the observation of many intelligent readers and writers. I want to thank my brother, Daniel, who has probably read more versions of this novel than anyone else. Endless gratitude to Randy Nikkel Schroeder, whose Directed Writings course taught me more about the process than I can ever express, and thanks as well to Kit Dobson, who offered valuable feedback on one of the earliest drafts. Thanks also to Niall Howell, Tomas Boudreau, and Tom Hubschmid, who read with openness, keenness, and interest.

Shout-out to Scarlett R. Algee and the folks at JournalStone for taking the chance on a pessimistic, quasi-cosmic coming-of-age horror novel about suburban violence, addiction, and masculine conditioning. And to Sean Leonard, too: your eye for editing is sharp.

Thank you to Sophy Romvari for your love and artistic insight. Same goes for my family.

It's impossible to acknowledge everyone, but to all those who have been there from the beginning to the end, I appreciate you.

About the Author

Photo by Robert Boschman

MIKE THORN IS THE AUTHOR OF the short story collection *Darkest Hours*. His fiction has appeared in numerous magazines, anthologies and podcasts, including *Vastarien*, *Dark Moon Digest*, *The NoSleep Podcast*, *Prairie Gothic*, and *Beyond the Book of Eibon*. His film criticism has been published in *MUBI Notebook*, *The Film Stage*, and *Vague Visages*. He completed his M.A. with a major in English literature at the University of Calgary, where he wrote a thesis on epistemophobia in John Carpenter's *Prince of Darkness*.

CPSIA information can be obtained
at www.ICGtesting.com
Printed in the USA
FSHW010459020721
82904FS

9 781950 305605